"You're not even breathing hard."

Drew's words were accusing, but his eyes were inviting.

Wrong, Cassie thought, her heart pounding with excitement. But to him she said, "Don't worry, you'll get the hang of the game. You've got a lot of natural ability."

"Oh?" He grinned slowly and patted the floor next to him. "Have a seat and tell me about it."

The sight of him, tousled and perspiring, roused an urgency in Cassie that she wasn't sure she could handle. "I think I'll get a drink of wat—"

"Later." His moist palm connected with hers, and he pulled her downward. "Eventually I might learn how to play recquetball, Cassie, but I know another sport that's loads more fun...."

Vicki Lewis Thompson began her writing career at the age of eleven with a short story in the *Auburn Illinois Weekly* and quickly became a byline junkie. Then she discovered she could write books—and she's written a lot of them! In the year 2000, Vicki saw her fiftieth book on the shelves. Vicki lives in Tucson, Arizona, and has two grown children and a husband who encourages her to write from the heart.

VICKI LEWIS THOMPSON

Cupid's Caper

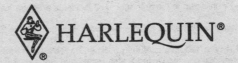

HARLEQUIN®

TORONTO • NEW YORK • LONDON
AMSTERDAM • PARIS • SYDNEY • HAMBURG
STOCKHOLM • ATHENS • TOKYO • MILAN • MADRID
PRAGUE • WARSAW • BUDAPEST • AUCKLAND

To Demetra Tims,
a master graphoanalyst and a dynamite lady,
and to my own friendly carrier, Rudy

ISBN 0-373-63178-2

CUPID'S CAPER

Copyright © 1987 by Vicki Lewis Thompson.

This edition published by arrangement with Harlequin Books S.A.

® and TM are trademarks of the publisher. Trademarks indicated with ® are registered in the United States Patent and Trademark Office, the Canadian Trade Marks Office and in other countries.

Visit us at www.eHarlequin.com

Printed in U.S.A.

1

THE LIST OF ELIGIBLE MEN was dwindling fast.

Cassie wheeled the postal-service Jeep into the circular drive with determined optimism. Today for certain she would corner the top candidate on that list, Dr. Andrew W. Bennett IV. The sky was too blue, the September sun too bright for another failure.

"Four mornings in a row you've been gallivanting around," she muttered to the invisible owner of the expensive adobe home. "These are your golden years. Seems to me you should relax, polish the Mercedes, gossip with the postman. Or in this case, postwoman."

She braked the white Jeep to a stop and picked up the large package beside her. She'd made it big on purpose—too big to fit into the rural-style mailbox out by the street. But her quarry hadn't cooperated. She was tired of smuggling the package back into her car every night and out to the Jeep the next morning.

What if he was bedridden? The thought hadn't occurred to her before. No, he couldn't be. He belonged to an aircraft owners' association, and he wouldn't keep that up if he didn't own and fly a plane, would he?

Maybe he spent all his time taking Albuquerque's single women to lunch. Or they took him? Unmarried retired gentlemen were in short supply these days. If they weren't, she wouldn't need to help Grammy Jo find a boyfriend.

Well, so what if Grammy Jo had lots of competition for Dr. Bennett's attentions? She could handle it. But she'd never have the chance if Cassie couldn't find the elusive doctor at home long enough to do a little surreptitious matchmaking.

Holding the light package in one hand, Cassie rang the doorbell and listened for footsteps. When she heard them, she wanted to shout for joy. At last!

Then the door opened, and her excitement evaporated. The man standing in the doorway couldn't possibly be Dr. Andrew W. Bennett IV.

"I have a package for Dr. Bennett," she said dully, cursing her misfortune. All this work, and someone else answered the door. A houseguest, probably. Maybe his son was visiting for a few days. Handsome guy. Nicely trimmed beard and mustache. If he was related to Dr. Bennett, that was encouraging. The good doctor might be easy on the eyes as well as rich. But she still wanted to meet the old guy himself, not some go-between.

The man's brown eyes reflected curiosity as he took the bulky carton from Cassie and studied the mailing label. "I wonder who's sending me a package."

Cassie stared at him. Apparently he hadn't understood that the package wasn't his.

"No return address, and it's light as a feather." He smiled. "Could be a joke. Some of my friends have a weird sense of humor."

"You misunderstood me. This is addressed to Dr. Andrew W. Bennett IV." She pointed to her own large script on the package. "Is he home?" Maybe she could maneuver the situation yet. "I figured out that he's a psychologist, and I have a question about this friend of mine..."

The man glanced up. For some reason this cute little bundle of a mailperson wanted a psychologist. *Everyone expects free advice,* he thought. And the "I have a friend" line was the oldest one in the book. "Do you have some problem you'd like to discuss?"

"No, not me," she said hastily. "But my friend— I'd like to talk to Dr. Bennett, if he's at home."

Why was she so sure he wasn't Dr. Bennett? He decided to play along for the hell of it. "Would you like to make an appointment?"

"He still takes regular appointments?"

"Last I heard." He liked the way her strawberry-blond hair escaped from its arrangement on top of her head and tumbled like miniature Slinky toys against her neck.

"Oh." She frowned. "I guess psychologists don't have to retire at a certain age like the rest of us."

He peered at her in confusion. Maybe she did have a problem. She wasn't making much sense at the moment. He wished he could see her eyes better, but the sunglasses hid both color and expression. "I don't understand."

"I expected Dr. Bennett to be retired."

He passed a hand over his face and looked at her warily. "What difference does it make whether I—I mean he—is retired?" There was a moment of silence. Then he knew from her quick intake of breath that she'd figured out her mistake.

A red flush spread slowly from her neck to her cheeks. "You're Dr. Andrew W. Bennett IV."

He nodded.

"Damn, how could I goof up like that? I thought you were at least sixty-five."

"And I imagined I was holding up pretty well for my age. Obviously I've been deluding myself."

"Oh, no! You look fine. It was the magazine."

"What magazine?"

"The one for senior citizens. You know, *Inspired Retirement*. It came addressed to you. I'm sure it did."

He chuckled. "I'm beginning to understand. I subscribed to that for my grandfather."

"He lives here, too?"

"He lives in Phoenix."

"Oh."

He couldn't for the life of him figure out why she was so desperate to meet his grandfather, but she was obviously crushed that the older man lived several hundred miles away.

"If he lives in Phoenix," she persisted, "why does the magazine have your address on it?"

"The subscription department got some wire crossed. He's Dr. Andrew W. Bennett II, and they got us mixed up. I've called them about it." He rubbed his knuckles across his beard and regarded her thoughtfully. "Now that my ego's back in shape, how about your friend's problem? Would you like an appointment, or does the fact that I'm thirty-one ruin everything?"

"I don't need an appointment, and yes, I'm afraid you're far too young." She sighed and dropped her gaze to the brick sidewalk beneath her feet.

"Uh-oh. My ego's in danger again. I assure you I've had years of training. I'm a competent psychologist."

"I'm sure you are."

He wondered if she did need counseling and couldn't afford it. Maybe she thought someone who was retired wouldn't charge as much. "I operate on a sliding scale. We can work out a fee that you could handle," he said gently.

She glanced up. "I don't need counseling."

"What about your friend?" He felt a growing need to help, although he hadn't the slightest idea what was wrong.

"She doesn't need counseling, either."

"Then what does she need?"

Her expression was unreadable. "Someone older," she said at last, turning quickly toward the Jeep. "Enjoy your package," she added, hopping into the driver's seat, which was on the right-hand side.

Her answer made him even more worried about her grasp on reality. He couldn't let her leave like this. After all, there was his professional pride to consider, his vow to help troubled psyches. "Wait," he called above the sound of the Jeep's engine.

She touched her foot to the brake.

"I have a few letters ready to mail. If you'll hold on a minute, I'll get them."

She nodded, and he left the door open while he dashed to his study. Thank God he did have some letters ready to go. Should he ask her in for coffee? Maybe not today. Too pushy. But in a few days he could casually watch for her Jeep, wander out to the mailbox and strike up a conversation.

Letters in hand, he went back out the open door. "Here they are." He strode toward the Jeep holding three business envelopes. He could feel her watching him.

"Ever played racquetball?" she asked, taking the envelopes.

"No." He decided she definitely needed his help. Racquetball? How had that subject arisen? But he'd take whatever opening she gave him to get past her reticence, her reluctance to admit she needed professional guidance with her problem, whatever it was. "Do you play?"

"Every chance I get. Smashing that rubber ball is terrific for working out frustrations. You should consider it. You have a great build for the game." She put the Jeep in gear and started to pull away.

"Wait!"

Once more she braked. "More letters?"

"No. I, uh, I've always meant to try racquetball."

"Good. You'll like it." She smiled at him. "See you later, Dr. Bennett."

He had his mouth open to suggest that she teach him the fundamentals of the game, but she was gone. Damn. He should have been more forthright. But he'd been afraid he might scare her away.

He watched the Jeep swerve next to his neighbor's mailbox. She jerked the metal flap open with practiced ease and stuffed the mail inside. He wondered how long she'd been on this route. He'd never noticed her before, but then how many times had he looked carefully at the person delivering the mail? Most days he wasn't even home when it arrived.

She was a strange one, all right. Nevertheless, she had an intriguing smile, sort of like a mischievous kid's. The dimples probably contributed to that impression because she was no kid. The blue-gray uniform of shorts and a button-up shirt wasn't glamorous, but she did special things for it.

Of course, her cute little figure was beside the point. His interest in her was that of a mental-health professional concerned with a troubled mind. The body that went with it wasn't under consideration. But then again...

Nope, she was definitely not his type. Couldn't be an inch over five foot. She'd have to stand on a box to kiss him. He grinned. Not a bad image. Glancing once more in the direction taken by the white Jeep, he walked back into the house.

WITH A SNAP OF HER WRIST, Cassie sent the blue ball hurtling toward the front wall of the court. It hit an inch above the floor and flew back, an impossible target for her opponent.

"Damn that killer shot of yours!" Ruth dragged the sweatband at her wrist across her forehead. "Let's rest."

"You rest. I'll practice."

"Good idea. Maybe you'll get this Dr. Bennett business out of your system and you won't be so rough on me."

"It's not fair, that's all." Cassie smashed the ball against the front wall and began volleying with herself while Ruth leaned her lanky frame against the side of the racquetball court.

"All my careful work," Cassie complained. "How could I know some stupid magazine employee would foul me up like that?" Her words and the hollow whack of the ricocheting ball echoed in the narrow cement enclosure. "Andrew Bennett had the perfect slant to his writing—kind yet levelheaded. And his *m*'s and *n*'s were wonderful. Grammy Jo loves men with exploratory, probing minds."

"You'll find someone else. I have faith." Ruth refastened the elastic holding her dark hair in a ponytail.

"Thanks, but his type is unusual. Strong emotion, determination. I could strangle him for being so young."

"There must be others on your route. Weren't there a couple of promising single men on another street?"

"Yes, but neither of their handwriting samples compared to Bennett's. Once that *Inspired Retirement* magazine arrived, I studied him inside and out. You should see the dots over his *i*'s. He's loyal beyond belief. His *d* stems show pride and dignity, and the crossbars on his *t*'s are loaded with enthusiasm." She pounded the ball again.

"Speaking of enthusiasm, Cassie, I haven't heard you speak so enthusiastically about a man in months."

"He was perfect for Grammy Jo."

"How about for Cassie?"

Cassie missed the hurtling ball. "I...I hadn't even thought about it." Which wasn't exactly true. Andrew Bennett had been on her mind all day. "Right now I'm concentrating on Grammy Jo's situation."

"Does that mean you're not giving up the quest?"

Cassie paused and caught the bouncing ball in her free hand before winking at her friend. "You know me better than that."

Ruth shrugged. "You seem so hung up on this Bennett character I thought he'd spoiled you for anyone else."

"He's only a setback. He may have been good, but I'll find somebody better. Maybe I'll ask for a transfer to a different route." *But then I'd never see Andrew Bennett again.*

"You're sure this handwriting analysis thing is foolproof?"

"Ruth, nothing is foolproof, but I'll bet that I learn more about someone from a signature than others would by watching an in-depth video interview of a person, like they do with those computer dating services. I consider my methods an effective screening device."

"Your grandmother would have a fit if she found out what you're up to."

Cassie grinned. "And unless I let you win the next game, you'll tell her, right?"

"Could be, champ."

"No, you won't, Ruth."

"How can you be so sure?"

"I've analyzed your handwriting, too." Cassie served the ball to Ruth's backhand with competitive glee. The racquetball match was working its magic, taking away the tension of her miserable failure today with the undercurrent of emotion that her encounter with Bennett had produced.

Tomorrow she'd zero in on the next name on the list. Dr. Andrew W. Bennett IV wasn't the only fish in the sea or eligible bachelor on her mail route. She'd be better off forgetting about him for the time being.

As she drove down his street the next morning, however, she couldn't dismiss him quite so easily, especially with him standing next to his mailbox. What did he want? Could he have somehow guessed about the package?

His beard shone glossy and rich in the morning sunshine. The dark color contrasted with his turquoise shirt of fashionably wrinkled cotton, which stretched across his broad shoulders. Casually he leaned tanned forearms on the mailbox and watched her approach. His arms looked strong, good for racquetball. Also good for— She swallowed nervously and stopped the Jeep.

"Hello again," she said with a quick smile. She mustn't act the least bit guilty.

"Good morning." He smiled, too, but his brown gaze was speculative as he walked up next to the Jeep. "The package was empty."

"Empty? My goodness, how odd. Here's your mail, Dr. Bennett."

"Thanks." He made no **move** to take the outstretched bundle of letters **and** circulars. "At first I thought it might be from one of my crazy friends. I do a lot of work with the inmates of several prisons, and some of my clients love practical jokes."

"How interesting." And she was interested. Collecting information on his career was fascinating when she already knew so much about his personality. But she also had to get out of here. Discussing yesterday's package wasn't a good idea, no matter how many tidbits about Andrew Bennett's life were dropped along the way. "I'm on a tight schedule, Dr. Bennett, so if you don't mind taking your mail, I'll be on my way." She shoved the bundle forward, almost touching his chest.

He folded his arms and planted his feet wide apart, obviously there to stay awhile. "But then I looked at the handwriting and realized the inmates I know are all men, and I'd swear that a woman addressed the package. Besides, it was mailed right here in Albuquerque."

"Undoubtedly an accomplice," she said, wiggling the letters in front of him.

"That's possible, but I have another theory." He squinted against the morning sun. "I think you sent me that empty package."

"Why on earth would I do that?"

"To meet me."

"What an absurd idea." She felt the flush spreading across her cheeks, knew it was giving her away to someone trained in reading people's reactions. But she was telling the truth. The package was the most absurd idea she'd ever had, and she wished to God she'd never sent it.

"What's your name?"

"Why?" She squirmed in the seat and looked away. He was going to report her for unprofessional behavior.

"Because we have more to discuss, and I'd like to use your name while we do it."

She sighed and laid her forehead on the steering wheel. "My name is Cassie Larue, and yes, I sent the package."

He rested his hands against the roof of the Jeep and leaned closer. "Do you need to see a psychologist, Cassie?"

Her head jerked up. "No!"

"If you keep denying it, you'll never work out your problems. I won't charge you for the first session. Does that help?"

"I don't need a psychologist," she insisted through clenched teeth.

"Yet you sent the package deliberately so you could meet me."

"Yes, but I thought you'd be older."

He pushed himself away from the Jeep in exasperation. "Here we go again. What the hell does my age have to do with this?"

She was trapped. The truth was the only way out, but she cringed at the prospect of telling it. Confiding in Ruth was one thing, but this man was a complete stranger. Well, not exactly a stranger. She remembered the slant of his handwriting—a kind man. He wouldn't make fun of her or her grandmother.

"Okay." She shut her eyes and spoke rapidly. "I'm looking for someone for my grandmother. She's a widow and lonely, and when you're sixty-eight, you don't exactly cruise the bars. Besides, single men of her age are snapped up so quickly, and she's not very aggressive about finding another husband." She opened one eye and peeked at him. His lips were pressed together, and little crinkles had appeared at the corners of his eyes, but he wasn't going to let himself laugh, she could tell. She liked him very much for that.

"So you're scouting around for her?" His voice betrayed a hint of a chuckle, and he quickly cleared his throat.

"Very quietly, yes." Cassie's trust in him grew. Her plan was outrageous. Even Ruth, her best friend, had said so. But he was listening with calm consideration and trying to keep his amusement to himself.

"How did I become a candidate?"

"All the single men on my route are candidates. It

occurred to me that I knew a lot about the people that I serve. That's what makes the job interesting, noticing letters they receive and send and the publications they subscribe to."

"Like *Inspired Retirement*." His eyes danced with merriment.

Cassie grinned, and he took that as his signal that it was okay to smile. It was a nice moment, a shared little joke. Cassie began to enjoy herself. He did have beautiful eyes, and the rest of him wasn't bad, either. "You have to admit that that magazine interpretation was an honest mistake."

"I can see how you were misled, Cassie."

"I knew you were single and a psychologist and a pilot, right?" She looked to him for confirmation.

"Yes on all counts. I'm divorced, a consulting psychologist for several prison systems in the Southwest, and I use my Cessna to visit each facility."

Divorced. Cassie wondered briefly what could possibly go wrong in a marriage with such a kind, considerate man. "I've been waiting for weeks to catch a glimpse of you so I'd know your age, but when the magazine came, I figured you were retired. The perfect man for Grammy Jo. I mailed you a package so I could see for sure if you were or not." She decided not to tell him about the handwriting analysis. Some psychologists she'd met didn't think much of her craft.

"You were lucky to find me home."

"Yes, I was." Nor did he need to know how many other times she had tried to deliver that package.

"Well, I'm almost sorry to be thirty-one instead of seventy, Cassie. Your grandmother must be a wonderful woman if you're going to all this trouble for her."

"She is." Cassie held out his mail again. "Here you are. I really must be on my way."

This time he took the bundle. "Thanks for your honesty, Cassie. And good luck with your hunt. If I hear of a good prospect, I'll let you know."

"Thanks." She didn't believe he'd find her any prospects, but it was nice of him to say he might. She gazed into his smiling face one more time. "I appreciate your understanding, Dr. Bennett."

"That sounds pretty formal after all we've shared in the past two days. My name's Drew."

"Drew." She turned the name over in her mind, merging it with the picture of him she'd been building for several weeks. "Drew's nice. Fits you much better than Andy."

He laughed. "I couldn't be Andy. That's my dad, Andrew W. Bennett III."

"Don't all these men with the same name cause a lot of confusion?"

"Obviously to the subscription department at *Inspired Retirement*."

"What name does your grandfather use?"

"He's always been called A.W. And I think my great-grandfather was known as Junior. My great-great-grandfather, who started the whole thing, wouldn't tolerate anything less than Andrew. No nicknames for him."

"That means if you carry on the tradition, your son will be Andrew W. Bennett V," she said lightly, "and you're about out of nicknames." She paused in sudden embarrassment. "Unless you've already..."

"No, I haven't already." He looked at her, and a sad expression flitted across his face. "We didn't get around to that. Probably just as well under the circumstances, but..."

"You'd be a good father."

"Oh? What makes you think so?"

"Your down—" she caught herself before she said "downstrokes" "—down-to-earth attitude," she finished, almost choking as she realized the wealth of misinterpretation that could have been caused by her first choice of words. She'd better leave before she really put her foot in her mouth. "I ought to deliver the rest of this mail before the sun sets."

"How does that line go? 'Neither rain, nor sleet, nor—'"

"Nor fascinating conversation with a customer," she finished hurriedly. "Goodbye, Drew."

"Goodbye, Cassie." For the second time in two days, he watched her careen down the street, weaving from mailbox to mailbox. So she wasn't mentally unbalanced at all; she was acting as matchmaker for her grandmother.

He found her project endearing. He found her even more endearing. Today her tiny stature didn't loom as quite such an obstacle. If they did match up, he'd hold her off the ground. She couldn't weigh over a hundred pounds, and at one time he'd been able to bench-press two hundred and twenty.

If he could come up with a prospective boyfriend for her grandmother, that would give them a reason to talk again. No, bad idea. Besides, he'd have to meet the grandmother before he'd consider getting involved. Maybe he'd just ask Cassie out. Why help her play cupid and complicate everything?

His recommendation for a boyfriend might not work

out, and any problems could ruin his chance of a relationship with Cassie. He didn't know anyone, anyway. He stopped walking as a thought struck him with the force of a wrecking ball. He did know someone. He most certainly did.

2

DREW GAVE HIMSELF some time to think about the idea. Work kept him out of town for two days, and flying alone in the Cessna for several hours provided a chance to examine the possibilities. He wouldn't help matchmake just to get the inside track with Cassie. That wouldn't be fair to anyone involved.

But suppose Grammy Jo—he smiled at the rosy-cheeked and bespectacled image the name conjured up—was a dynamite lady? A.W. had been flitting from woman to woman in the past few years and had admitted recently that they all bored him.

On Friday morning Drew canceled his morning appointments, and when he heard the distinctive braking and acceleration of the postal Jeep, he ambled out to the road.

Cassie saw him when she was two houses away, and her heart beat faster. Each morning she'd anticipated this possibility, and each morning she'd been disappointed. Until now.

She checked in the Jeep's side-view mirror and wished her lipstick had lasted. Her hair was in disarray, as always, from the breeze that blew through the open right-hand door. Ordinarily she didn't care how tousled she looked, but at the moment she longed for a place to hide and freshen up.

He stood by the road, hands in his pockets, while she

delivered his neighbor's mail. She came close to dropping several letters as her gaze kept darting to the man waiting for her a few yards away. She snapped the mailbox closed, took a deep breath and drove toward him.

"Hi." He placed both hands on the roof of the Jeep and leaned down until his face was even with hers.

"Hi, yourself." Cassie's hands trembled as she gathered his mail. For several days she'd been telling herself he really wasn't very good-looking. She'd been lying.

When he smiled, his even teeth were incredibly white when outlined by the sable luxury of his beard. And his eyes—intelligent, caring and loaded with sex appeal. "Looks like a lot of hunk, er, junk today," she said, riffling through the stack of envelopes in an embarrassed gesture. Good Lord, what would he think of her?

Apparently he hadn't heard or was too kind to acknowledge her Freudian slip. "I'm curious as to whether you analyze the kind of junk mail people get. For instance, is mine the same kind you deliver to the Harrisons next door?"

She glanced up through her dark glasses, allowing herself the pleasure of looking him over without being caught at it. She wasn't sure yet what to do about the excitement he stirred in her. "No, your junk isn't average." She doubted anything about him was average. "You get more charity appeals than anyone else on the street."

Drew groaned. "That doesn't surprise me."

"And you give to all those causes, too."

"You noticed that?"

"Of course. It was one of the reasons I picked you."
She held on to the envelopes a moment longer before
reluctantly handing them to him. She didn't want to
end the encounter quite yet.

Drew took the mail but made no attempt to leave.
"Cassie, what does your grandmother look like?"

Thank God for dark glasses, Cassie thought, shocked
by the question. Was Drew out there because he was
willing to consider dating Grammy Jo? "She's very attractive," Cassie said as evenly as possible. "But she is
sixty-eight years old. I really don't think the two of you
would—"

"Not for me," he said quickly, laughing.

"Oh." Cassie sighed with relief. "Then why the
question?"

"I just—Could you park that thing and come in for a
cup of coffee? I think we have something to discuss."

"I, ah, let's see." She glanced at her watch, stalling
for time. She hadn't expected this to happen. He'd
taken her project seriously and wanted to suggest
someone for her grandmother. And that meant an in-
evitable escalation of her own relationship with this
handsome psychologist. Was that what she wanted?
Yes, perhaps it was.

"I promise not to keep you from your appointed
rounds. Just one cup of coffee."

She responded to the gentle persuasion in his voice.
If that was the tone he used with his clients, he had to
be very successful, indeed. "I guess fifteen or twenty
minutes won't ruin my schedule."

His invitation sounded casual enough, and her ac-
ceptance was equally offhand, but Cassie felt as if she'd
jumped from a plane with no parachute.

"You can park in the driveway." He led the way toward the house, and she followed in the Jeep.

Drew watched her climb out of the vehicle and walk toward him. She *was* short but beautifully built. The sunlight made her hair shine like polished bronze, and the gamine smile flashed again, complete with dimples. What a little firecracker. "Have you lived here long?" he asked, holding the door open for her.

"I thought you wanted to know about my grandmother."

"I do. I was making polite conversation."

"Is that right?" She took off her dark glasses and slid them on top of her head before turning to look at him.

Hazel eyes. Clear and trusting. He couldn't meet those eyes and tell a fib. "No, not really. I'd like to know more about you, too." He saw the flicker of understanding in her gaze. And something more. Permission to pursue her a little.

"I came to Albuquerque and moved in with my grandparents five years ago during my abortive college career."

"Abortive?"

"I couldn't settle on a major, so I quit after two years and got a job with the post office. Soon after that Grandpa died, so I decided to stay at the house to keep Grammy Jo company."

"You don't find living with her sort of—" he searched for a tactful way to say it "—sort of confining for you?"

"No."

Okay, Bennett, where do you go from here? He fell back on his old standby from counseling sessions. "I see."

Her dimples flashed at him. "No, you don't. You think it's a weird arrangement."

"I'm sure you have your reasons."

"I do. Number one, I love her. Number two, she's good company. Number three, she's a convenient excuse if I don't want to spend the night with a man."

Right between the eyes. Whamo. "I see," he said again, not able to come up with anything better.

"There's a lot of sexual pressure on a single woman these days."

"I guess so." Well, at least he knew she was choosy. That was okay as long as she felt inclined to choose him. Because he'd already decided to make a play for Cassie Larue. Closing the front door, he motioned to the right. "The kitchen's in there. Have a seat at the counter, and I'll get the coffee."

Cassie could have predicted the neatness of the kitchen from his handwriting. The tile was Mexican but done in subdued shades of brown, not the usual bright colors found south of the border. The room was cool. He must have central air.

She perched on a stool and rested her chin on her hands while Drew poured two mugs of coffee from a full glass pot.

"Cream or sugar?"

"No, thanks." Cassie accepted the steaming mug. "The coffee was all made, Drew," she chided him. "This wasn't a spur-of-the-moment idea, was it?"

"No." He sat across from her at the kitchen bar. "You intrigue me, Cassie. I really did invite you in to talk about your grandmother. But I won't say that's the only reason."

"Fair enough." She sipped her coffee with great care

and thought she was glad to have made that statement about her reasons for living with her grandmother. Now she had room to maneuver. "Who do you have in mind for Grammy Jo?"

"Maybe my grandfather."

She raised her eyebrows. "Another Andrew W. Bennett?"

"Yes, but I'm not ready to suggest that they meet. I need to know some things first."

"Is this the one called A.W. who lives in Phoenix?"

"That's him."

"But if he's in Phoenix and Grammy Jo is here, I don't see how—"

Drew waved one hand. "I thought of that, but it's a minor obstacle, really. Bringing them together in the first place might be tricky."

"No kidding. I didn't even consider extending this search nationwide."

"We can handle the meeting, though. We'll think of something. And if they hit it off... Remember both these people are retired, and either of them could move with enough motivation."

"Hold the wedding bells, Drew. I don't know anything about your grandfather."

"And I don't know anything about your grandmother, except her name and your assessment of her looks. And the word *attractive* isn't very specific. Is she tall, or short like you?"

"Tall. Five foot eight, I think."

"That's good. A.W.'s six foot, and he likes his ladies tall. Does she have a nice figure?"

Cassie's eyes snapped open. "Does A.W?"

Drew chuckled. "He doesn't have a potbelly, if that's what you mean."

"Neither does Grammy Jo, if that's what you mean."

"Hair?"

"Yes."

Drew shook his head and frowned. "I meant the style, Cassie. I assume she'd not bald."

"Which is more than I can assume about A.W."

"Do you want to consider this or not?"

Cassie took a deep breath and folded her arms on the counter. "Not if we're going to grade them like merchandise at a swap meet."

He met her gaze. "Okay. But you know as well as I do that looks are important when you're thinking of introducing two strangers. If they had time to get to know each other, it would be different, but they won't have that kind of time if they don't hit it off at first."

"You're right. But tell me some other things about A.W. besides his looks. Something real."

He considered for a moment, rubbing his beard with his knuckles. "Well, I think he's a great guy, but you'll cancel my opinion for being prejudiced. He used to be a surgeon, made a lot of money at it. Dad was his only child, and I was the only male grandchild. My father rebelled against medicine as a career." Drew smiled in self-mockery. "Maybe to rebel against my dad, I took A.W. as my role model. I chose psychology instead of surgery, but I've still patterned myself after my grandfather. I admire his style, his zest for life."

Cassie tried to get a mental picture of A.W. Grammy Jo needed someone with zest, that was for sure. "He's a widower?"

"For the past six years. He loves to dance and play

golf, even rides horses. He's had lots of female friends since my grandmother died. He can go out as much as he—"

Cassie held up one hand. "You don't have to tell me that. At his age the women far outnumber the men. If he's already got ladies coming out his ears, why introduce him to Grammy Jo?"

"A hunch. I don't think he's found anyone to compare with my grandmother, and he's lonely. If your Grammy Jo is anything like you, she might be the answer, but I'd like to meet her before we consider going further with this thing. I'll know, once I see her and talk to her, whether she'd be right for A.W."

Cassie put down her mug with a firm click. "Just a minute. Grammy Jo may be wonderful for your grandfather, but that doesn't mean I'll approve of him for Grammy Jo!"

"I know." He refilled her cup without asking. "One thing at a time. The easiest first step is for me to meet your grandmother, and then we'll see if we want to continue from there. What do you say?"

"I'm thinking." Cassie surrounded the warm mug with both hands and stared into the dark liquid. "Suddenly I'm very nervous about this scheme. It sounded terrific when I first started my search, but now we're talking about the possibility of bringing two people together for real." She glanced up and met his gaze. God, but his eyes were marvelous. "What if it's a terrible mistake?"

"Look, we won't be making any decisions for them, only creating a situation that gives them more options. Without our interference these two people would never know each other. What if they'd be perfect companions?"

"If you meet Grammy Jo, I don't want her to suspect what's going on. How can we set that up?"

"You said you live with her. I could take you out." He studied her over the rim of his coffee cup.

"Or pretend to. You don't really have to follow through. You could let me out on the corner."

"Cassie, I'd enjoy spending the evening with you, even without the impetus of this other business. I thought I made that clear earlier."

"Just testing the water."

"The water's fine." He held her gaze for a long moment. "Do you already have a date tonight?"

"No."

"Do you expect your grandmother to be home?"

"As far as I know. We were going to watch a movie on television."

"Then it's settled. I'll pick you up at six-thirty for dinner."

Cassie grew a little bolder. "Forget dinner. I have a better idea."

"Oh?"

"Forget that, too," she said, arching one brow. She was relaxing in his presence, easing into a bit of flirtation.

"Aw, shucks."

She could tell he hadn't accepted her rejection. Well, she hadn't really meant it as such either.

"If we can't do that and we can't have dinner," he teased, "what's left?"

"What a limited repertoire you have." Cassie was enjoying herself.

"Expand it for me."

"Okay. I'll teach you to play racquetball."

"That sounds very unromantic, Cassie. And I don't have a racquet."

"I have a spare. Come on, a fast game would be good for you. You're too intense about your work, and you don't relax and forget it often enough."

"How do you know? I doubt if you can decipher that information from my mail."

Cassie fumbled for an answer. "You don't subscribe to any sports magazines." She'd tell him about the handwriting sometime, especially now that they were embarking on this new venture. But she wasn't ready yet. "Would you like to learn something about racquetball?"

He shrugged. "Sure, why not? Someone once told me I have a good build for it. Of course, I know nothing about the game, so maybe I shouldn't feel complimented by that remark."

"It was a compliment." She gulped the last of her coffee and scooted off the stool. "And I've got to go."

"How about the address?"

"Oh, right." She spied a pad of paper and a pen by the kitchen telephone. "Here's where Grammy Jo lives," she said, scribbling the directions. "How much time do you want with her?"

"Ten minutes is plenty for now. I'll arrive at six-thirty, and you can stay hidden away, pretending to be late, until six-forty. Unless you're usually right on time for your dates. I wouldn't want her to get suspicious."

She tilted her head. "Guess whether I am or not, Mr. Psychologist."

"All right. I'll guess, Cassie Larue, that you keep those men cooling their heels on a regular basis."

"Good guess."

"And that's fine this time. We have a purpose. But next time I'd appreciate more promptness."

"What makes you think there will be a next time?"

"What makes you think there won't?"

She remembered his long, firm downstrokes—determination was strong in him. "Maybe you won't care for my grandmother."

"Your grandmother isn't the only reason we're going out, remember? We'll have other dates, Cassie. Count on it. And I hope you'll be on time."

"Why?"

"I can imagine the reason you keep men waiting, Cassie. I warn you, I won't be manipulated like that."

"A pip-squeak like me manipulate you? That's a laugh."

His lazy smile disconcerted her. "Oh, I think you'd try."

"Is that Dr. Bennett the psychologist talking?"

"Nope. Drew Bennett the man."

BY SIX-FIFTEEN THAT EVENING Cassie was dressed in white terry shorts and a pink T-shirt. *Dammit*, she cursed inwardly, *I'm ready early. I've never been ready early*. Who was this man who could cause her to race through her preparations for a date?

She stood in front of her bedroom mirror and adjusted her white headband. At least she'd be in control on the racquetball court. Drew had never played before, and she was fast becoming an excellent competitor. Of course, with the determination and tenacity

Drew revealed in his handwriting, he'd learn quickly. And he had good rhythm. That would help.

She sat on the edge of the bed and fidgeted with her white wristbands. She couldn't go into any other part of the house, or Grammy Jo would realize she was ready for the date and the ruse wouldn't work. There was no sound in the room other than the ticking of the bedside clock. And then a rock tune belted from the stereo in the living room.

Cassie stiffened. Grammy Jo was doing her aerobics! No doubt she was wearing her purple-and-yellow-striped leotard, the one that made her look like a psychedelic zebra, and her orange tights. Within ten minutes her hair would be plastered to her head with sweat.

But worst of all, once Grammy Jo started her half-hour program, she didn't stop for anything. She had once said the Russians could declare war, but she'd finish her aerobics, anyway. Cassie's plan for a quiet conversation between Drew and her grandmother had been blown to smithereens. Why cower in the bedroom now? She picked up the canvas bag containing both racquets and a can of balls and walked out the door toward the pounding music.

She leaned against the back of the couch and watched her grandmother moving with unabashed zeal to the wild beat. Grammy Jo waved but kept jumping around, making the purple and yellow stripes flash like neon lights. Cassie groaned in frustration. Trying to stop her grandmother's gyrations would be hopeless, but Cassie thought maybe she could head Drew off at the door.

As she walked toward it, the bell rang. Cassie hurried forward, determined to hustle Drew away before he came inside. They could reschedule this little charade or maybe forget it altogether. Come to think of it, Grammy Jo didn't sit still for quiet talks very often. Come to think of it, she didn't sit still at all, unless a Robert Redford movie was on, like tonight.

Cassie opened the door partway and started to step across the threshold, but Drew held his ground, and she stopped only inches from his chest.

"What are you doing answering the door?" he said in an undertone.

"Forget Plan A," Cassie said, breathing in the heady spice of his cologne. "Let's go."

"Why? What's that music? Is Grammy Jo having a party or something?"

"No, she's... Forget it." She backed up a step, which allowed her a view of his muscled thighs and calves. Nice legs.

"Dammit, Cassie. Is she in there or not?"

"She is. But she's busy."

"Doing what?"

Cassie met his demanding gaze and sighed. "Aerobics."

"You're kidding."

"Yes, I'm kidding. Let's leave."

"You're not kidding. Cassie, I have to see this."

Cassie stood in the doorway, considering. "Well, why not? I guess this is the real Grammy Jo, anyway." She lifted her chin. "And I'm proud of her, just the way she is." She stood back and ushered him into the room. "Grammy Jo, this is Drew Bennett!" she shouted above the music.

"Glad to meet you, Drew!" Grammy Jo yelled back breathlessly. Then she began a series of jumping jacks.

"My pleasure!" Drew grinned at her.

"You two have a good time! I'd stop and be sociable, but I can't interrupt my routine. Still have fifteen minutes," she said, panting.

"No problem. See you later." Drew steered Cassie back out the door and down the walk toward his tan Audi.

She didn't speak until they'd pulled away from the curb. "So that's that," she said, turning her palms up. "I should have known we were fooling ourselves about this matchmaking business. Still want to play racquetball?"

"Of course. Which way to the courts?"

"Down this street, take a left, then two rights." She rested her arm against the ridge of the open car window. "And don't feel bad about abandoning the plan for Grammy Jo and A.W."

"What are you talking about?"

"Be honest, Drew. You thought she looked ludicrous in that outfit, jumping around to music for teenagers. You're too kind to say so, but I realize—"

"You don't realize diddly-squat, lady."

Her head snapped around. "I beg your pardon?"

"I think Grammy Jo's great."

"You do?"

"Yep. I can hardly wait for A.W. to meet her. She'll knock his socks off."

"She will?" Cassie smiled. "Of course she will. I knew it all along."

"Sure you did. That's why you tried to barricade the door to keep me from meeting her."

"Well, I—"

"Never mind." His gaze left the road and flicked over Cassie. "I like seeing you in something besides that uniform. You look very nice tonight."

"Thanks."

"Your headband has me worried, though. Are we going to get serious about this game?"

"You bet. I don't like to do anything halfway."

He chuckled. "I'm delighted to hear it. Neither do I."

A zing of excitement skipped through Cassie's body like a ricocheting ball. "I brought an extra headband for you."

"Gonna make me sweat, huh?"

"Absolutely. Here's the park."

They checked in with the attendant and walked into a narrow cement enclosure. When Cassie closed the door behind them, she realized for the first time how intimate the court was, with its four walls reaching well above their heads. She was alone with this handsome, bearded man, shut away with him in a private little cubicle. The thought was exciting, if a bit unnerving.

"Here's your headband," she said, pulling it out of her bag and handing it to him. After he put it on, she eyed him critically. "That's better. You look good in sportswear. Don't you play anything?" She couldn't believe his chest was naturally so well muscled. His white T-shirt fit him like a second skin.

"A lesser man would make something out of that remark."

"You know what I mean."

"Yeah, I do," he conceded. "Let's see. I have a weight bench, but I don't lift as often as I should."

"Lifting weights is conditioning, not playing. What about a sport for fun?"

"I guess I don't have one, unless you count flying the plane. Or perhaps..."

"Okay, okay." She handed him a racquet. "Now this game is all in the wrist. You snap your wrist as you hit the ball, like this." She explained and demonstrated the basics of the swing while he watched.

He tried to keep his mind on what she was telling him, but every time she hit the ball, her rear end tightened deliciously beneath the white shorts. She was going to make him sweat, all right, being closed into this tiny space with her and having to pretend an interest in racquetball.

She turned back to him. "Get the idea?"

"Yep."

Cassie recognized the light in his eyes. "Drew, be serious."

"I'm very serious. I think I'm going to love this game."

"Then you must be ready to try a few shots." She tossed him the blue rubber ball, and he caught it deftly. His shoulder muscles rippled as he swung, and she was so busy watching him she almost forgot to return the serve.

As they continued to alternate shots, Cassie worked to keep the ball bouncing off the front wall to make it a better target. But Drew's inexperience soon had the shots careening off the side and back walls, and he was racing wildly around the court.

"Take it easy," she cautioned, expertly returning the ball to the front wall. "This game requires more finesse than brute strength."

"I can tell you this much—it's not helping my frustration level." He dove for a ball and missed, landing himself with a soft thud on the concrete.

"You okay?" Cassie caught the bounding ball and hurried to his side.

"I'm fine." He sat up slowly. "My ego's shot to hell, though. You're not even winded."

"You'll learn. You're really doing very well, considering. You have a lot of natural ability."

He gazed up at her. "And you have a lot of ability, period. I'm impressed."

"Thanks."

"You're welcome." He patted the cement floor next to him. "Have a seat and rest. I know you don't need it, but you can pretend to breathe hard and make me feel better."

Laughing, Cassie dropped down opposite him and stretched her legs beside his. Then she wheezed and panted dramatically. "Whew! Am I bushed."

"Don't overdo it."

"The drinking fountains are right outside, if that would help any."

"Okay." Drew didn't move. He was breathing evenly again, but his shirt was marked with a triangle of sweat in front, and his hair was damp.

The masculine scent of him was strong in Cassie's nostrils, and desire flamed with surprising quickness in her exercise-warmed body. Her urgent reaction embarrassed her. Afraid Drew would sense her immediate response to him, she started to stand. "I think I'll get a—"

He caught her wrist and gently pulled her down again. "In a minute." He reached over and toyed with a tendril of hair that had escaped from her headband to curl at the nape of her neck.

She watched his eyes, soft at first as he studied her face. Gradually the glow changed to something more fierce, and the fingers that had absently caressed her hair moved with definite purpose behind her neck and urged her forward. Fleetingly she wondered if he kissed as he wrote.

He did. His lips met hers deliberately. The beard she had longed to touch feathered her chin, and his mustache teased her upper lip. Without hesitation he coaxed her mouth open, and his tongue boldly explored the warm, secret recesses of her mouth. He kissed her with such assurance that it never occurred to Cassie to pull away or deny him what he sought.

When he released her, she was quivering. Mutely they gazed at each other, plumbing the depths of emotion in the other's eyes. Slowly he traced her lips with the tip of his finger.

"I may learn how to play racquetball, but I'll always be lousy at playing lovers' games," he said softly, searching her eyes for his answer. "I want you, Cassie. It doesn't have to be tonight, but if there's no chance for me, tell me now. Don't use living with your grandmother as an excuse to put me off. I can take the straight truth."

"I won't use Grammy Jo," she whispered.

"Good." He regarded her silently. "When do you want to meet my grandfather?" he said at last.

"I... Whenever we can arrange it, I guess."

"Why not take a couple of days off and fly to Phoenix with me?"

A couple of days. Overnight. Cassie trembled.

"We can stay with Gramps. He has a big house."

Cassie's trembling stopped. They wouldn't be alone as she had assumed. "Sounds fine."

"Not really. I don't know how well I'll be able to sleep knowing you're under the same roof with me."

Cassie saw the desire that flared his nostrils and heated his gaze, and she began to tremble again. Perhaps a chaperone wouldn't make any difference, after all.

3

"THIS SOUNDS SERIOUS," Grammy Jo observed, wandering into Cassie's room and perching on the bed while she packed. "One date and you're flying off to Phoenix with him."

"Oh, it's not that serious," Cassie hedged. "We'll be staying with his grandfather."

"Some old coot as a chaperone? That doesn't sound like any fun."

"I'm sure he's not an old coot."

"I'll bet he is. Most men my age are."

Here's hoping this one isn't, Cassie prayed silently. "I guess I'll find out," she said aloud.

"Well, phooey. Here I thought you had a chance to get away for a little hanky-panky."

"Grammy Jo!"

"Don't Grammy Jo me. An old lady must cramp your style, and if I had more gumption, I'd throw you out so you could have a little privacy."

"Don't be silly." Cassie stopped packing and sat down next to her grandmother. "I love staying here with you," she insisted, wrapping one arm around the older woman's shoulders. And she did. She was closer to Grammy Jo than to her parents, who traveled extensively and always seemed more interested in business and each other than their daughter.

Blue eyes undimmed by age scrutinized Cassie.

"When you're twenty-five, your significant other shouldn't be your grammy."

"I haven't found a better candidate." Cassie thought of Drew and wondered if her statement would be the same after this two-day trip.

"You won't find a better candidate unless you look. You haven't been looking since your grandpa died."

"Sure I have."

"No, you haven't. And all because you're afraid to leave me alone. Don't think I don't know that."

"Wait a min—"

"And I love you for it, but I can't have you sacrificing anymore. Maybe this trip will turn into something, Cassie, in spite of the grandfather hanging around. Drew's quite a hunk, in my opinion."

"Mine, too." Cassie gave her grandmother a quick hug and stood. She only had a few minutes to finish packing. As she rummaged through her closet, she wondered what Grammy Jo would say if she knew the real reason her granddaughter was going to Phoenix. Cassie cast a speculative look at the older woman.

"I like the romantic gleam in your eye, girl. Take that red eyelet sundress. It's sexy as hell."

"What language, Grammy Jo." Cassie unhooked the dress from the closet rod. Her grandmother was right. It was her sexiest outfit. The front laced from the waist up to the low-cut neckline, and Cassie wore the dress braless.

"I'm old enough to use any language I like, thank you. I'm enjoying this liberation stuff."

Cassie laughed. "That you are." She wondered if A.W. Bennett was equally liberated and would be able to handle the feisty woman. Since becoming a widow

Grammy Jo had gradually discarded her domestic role whereas most men her age expected a woman to keep house. Cassie zipped her suitcase closed. "All set."

Grammy Jo glanced at her digital watch. "And five minutes early. You've never been on time for a man."

"Yeah, I know."

"He turns you on, doesn't he, sweetheart?"

Cassie sighed. "Yes, I must admit he does."

"I'm glad." Grammy Jo stood to hug her granddaughter. "I have a good feeling about this one."

Me, too, Cassie thought as she returned her grandmother's hug. But unless A.W. worked out for Grammy Jo, how could Cassie allow anything to develop between her and Drew? She hadn't missed the flicker of anxiety on her grandmother's face at the idea of Cassie's finding a beau, despite the brave words about kicking her granddaughter out. If Cassie became seriously involved with a man, Grammy Jo would be terribly lonely, no doubt about it. She wouldn't let on, not wanting her needs to stand in the way of Cassie's happiness, but Cassie would know. A.W. had to be the answer. He just had to.

Later, as Cassie sat beside Drew in the tan Audi during the drive to the airport, she began having doubts about the entire scheme. An attraction between two people was a delicate matter. What made her think she could assess who was the right man for Grammy Jo?

Drew glanced at her. "I hope you don't mind, Cassie, but I scheduled a meeting for this afternoon with a colleague of mine at Arizona State University. He's been wanting to see me for some time."

"Of course I don't mind."

"I'm afraid the meeting's confidential, concerning

one of his clients. I'll be leaving you to your own devices for an hour or so."

"I'm a big girl."

"That depends on your definition."

"Look here, Drew. I will not tolerate short jokes."

"Uh-oh. She's touchy today, folks."

Cassie gripped the leather armrest. "I suppose I am. I've got the jitters."

"About what?"

"This business with Grammy Jo and A.W. Aren't we being presumptuous?"

"Probably. Still, I've thought about your grandmother's position, and it must be awkward for her, trying to meet the right man. Hell, dating's awkward for people our age, let alone someone in her sixties."

Cassie was fascinated by his statement. "You think dating is awkward? I've never heard a man admit that before."

"It's a well-kept secret. Once we all leave high school and college, the field really narrows. Meeting eligible women isn't easy."

"What about through your job?"

Drew grimaced. "Uh-uh. My job involves contact with male prison inmates, and my office is in my home. Not exactly an ideal setup for meeting single women, as I quickly learned after my divorce. Now you, on the other hand, see hundreds of people in the course of delivering mail."

Cassie heard his unspoken question. "I've never gone out with anyone on my route. Not until you."

"I'm surprised."

"On a driving route like mine, I don't meet as many people as you might think. Most of the people are at work, and in the neighborhoods where I deliver, many of them are married. Besides, I haven't really been paying attention for myself. Just for Grammy Jo."

"Why not for yourself?"

"I...I guess because I can't imagine leaving Grammy Jo alone if I became serious about someone."

"That doesn't sound fair to either one of you. Is she laying some guilt trip on you or something?"

Cassie bristled. "Certainly not. In fact, she's delighted I'm going away for a couple of days. She was disappointed that we'd be chaperoned," Cassie added, wanting Drew to know how modern her grandmother was.

"Uh...we won't."

"What do you mean, we won't?"

"Gramps is having the house sprayed for crickets. He's not staying there tonight, and neither can we. We'll have lunch with him, and then he's going to Wickenburg to see friends."

"Oh. Then what are we...?"

"I, um—" he flashed her a quick look "—I thought we'd stay in Phoenix."

"Where?"

"At the airport. In one of the hotels."

Cassie's heartbeat hammered in her ears. "But we could come back this afternoon, couldn't we?"

"Not too easily, considering my meeting with Evan. We could fly back after that, but it would be a long day."

She found herself using his phrase. "I see."

"Yes, you probably do." Drew turned into the entrance to the private airfield. "Now we have a chance to be alone tonight, on whatever terms we want."

"I'm not sure about how far we should allow ourselves..."

"To become involved?" He pulled the car into a parking space and switched off the engine. Slowly he turned in the seat, his dark eyes challenging her. "Okay, what's the problem?"

"I think it would be better if I got to know A.W. first and had some idea if things would work out between him and Grammy Jo before we—"

"I didn't think our relationship was dependent on theirs."

"It isn't exactly. Well, sort of."

"Cassie, don't buy trouble. Your grandmother and A.W. will be a great matchup. Trust me. Very soon you'll be able to stop putting your own life on hold."

"I am not putting my life on hold!"

"Aren't you?" Drew touched her shoulder. "I think you are."

"Well, you're wrong."

The drone of an airplane overhead was the only sound in the still morning as they looked into each other's eyes, trying to read the emotions reflected there.

"If so, you wouldn't be putting restrictions on what happens tonight."

"I don't have to prove anything to you."

"No, but it might be time to prove something to yourself."

"Such as?"

"Whether you're ready to grow up."

"Thank you, Mr. Psychologist!"

"Cassie—" he shook his head "I—shouldn't have said that."

"But it's what you think, isn't it?"

He moved his index finger along the tense ridge of her shoulder, and his voice was soothing. "I wonder if you're afraid to take a chance, afraid to find out if we'd be any good together. Because we might be, and then you'd have to consider whether to leave your safe world. You can't hide behind your grandmother forever, Cassie."

"I am not hiding. She needs me!" Cassie glared at him. How dared he psychoanalyze her. "I told you there was a lot of sexual pressure these days on single women, remember? Yours is the line that goes, 'Sleep with me, and I'll get rid of all your hang-ups, baby.'"

"No!" He withdrew his hand from her shoulder. "No, by God. I just want... Hell." He turned away and stared out the window.

Cassie tried to stay angry, but she couldn't. She remembered Drew's words about dating being awkward at any age. He was right. One minute she wanted him to rip off her clothes and make wild, crazy love to her, and the next she wanted him to be a tame, undemanding escort like the men she usually went out with.

Since her grandfather had died, she'd convinced herself that avoiding a physical relationship with a man was for her grandmother's sake. Maybe that wasn't entirely true. She'd had two lovers in her life, not enough to claim sexual sophistication but enough that she shouldn't be frightened by the prospect of a night with Drew Bennett.

But she was. Unless he considered her more than a temporary fling, she'd get hurt. She had tried to go to bed with someone just for the sake of sex, and it hadn't worked.

"Let's not decide anything right now," Drew said, opening his car door. "We've got time. The airport hotels aren't full in September, so we don't have to make an advance reservation." He stepped outside. "Come on. I'm going to teach you how to fly."

Cassie followed his lead and slowly got out of the car, but her mind was racing. She didn't have to go to Phoenix with this disturbing man. Grammy Jo would drive her home from the airport if she decided not to fly into the wild blue yonder with him.

Drew took the suitcases from the trunk and started for the office of the small airport. "Ever been up in a private plane?"

"No." Cassie walked beside him. She had to go into the office, anyway, to call Grammy Jo.

"You'll love it. There's a wonderful sense of freedom, of escape, up there. And the view is tremendous compared to a commercial flight, where you're too far away to see anything."

"Sounds nice." And it did, dammit. She had every reason to go and only one to stay. She was afraid that Drew Bennett's powerful personality would swallow her. His handwriting had revealed his determination, his capacity for deep, emotional experiences, his analytical mind. Cassie had enjoyed the prospect of matching this man with her grandmother and watching the sparks fly.

But dealing with him herself was a different matter. She'd been in control of every other man in her life, had wanted it that way. Drew was not like the others. Not at all.

Before she realized what was happening, they'd bypassed the office and were standing on the tarmac beside Drew's silver-and-white plane. "Don't you have to check with the people inside before we take off?"

"Nope. The plane's gassed up and ready to go." Drew stowed their luggage in a back compartment and unhooked the tie-downs from the wings and tail. "Climb aboard," he said, holding out his hand to help her up to the high seat.

She hesitated. She could still back out, but once they were in the air... "Parachutes don't go with this rig, I suppose."

"No. You have to trust your pilot."

Her gaze searched his. "Can I?"

"Yes."

Cassie put her hand in his. "All right," she said softly.

Drew had accurately predicted her reaction to the flight. The rumbling vibration of the Cessna as they roared down the runway hummed through her body, and as the plane left the ground, she clamped her arms to her sides to keep from spreading them wide in imitation of a soaring bird. This was flying!

The grid of Albuquerque's streets spread beneath them like loosely woven yarn on a giant loom. Gradually the plane left the city and the surrounding residential areas, where private swimming pools gleamed like bits of Navajo turquoise. Drew pointed the nose of the Cessna west, over stark bluffs and canyons swathed in pink-and-purple shadows by the early-morning sun.

When they were beyond the congested traffic surrounding Albuquerque, Drew pulled off his headset and touched Cassie's arm.

She took her gaze from the mesmerizing view and gave him a triumphant smile.

He beamed with satisfaction, and his voice rose above the loud buzz of the plane's single engine. "I knew you'd like it."

"How did you know that?"

"I'm not sure. Maybe from the way you zip around in that Jeep or the way you play racquetball. You've got adventure in your soul, Cassie."

She didn't respond to his statement. Maybe she did crave adventure, but not with men. Especially men like Drew. With him she felt like a craven coward.

She realized now why she'd suggested racquetball for their first date. With racquetball she was one up on him. Here, in the cockpit of his plane, he was the person in complete control, a powerful masculine force guiding them across the sky with deft assurance. Cassie was intimidated.

"Ready to take over?"

"I don't know anything about flying, Drew." She looked doubtfully at the small half-circle steering wheel in front of her.

"That's okay. I'll be right here. Just pretend you're driving a car, but watch that gauge to keep us level with the horizon. Don't make any rapid movements, and you'll be fine."

Tentatively she grasped the wheel in front of her, and Drew let go of his dual control. As the gauge indicated a slight tilt of the wings, she slowly corrected the angle of the plane. Eventually she relaxed and began to absorb the feel of the plane, the heady sense of defying gravity.

"You should see your face, Cassie. It's glowing."

"I could get hooked on this."

"Great! I'll take you up anytime. You teach me racquetball, and I'll teach you flying. That's a fair trade."

"Hardly. You can get into racquetball for a little less expense than I can take up flying."

"Cassie, I'm not going to charge you for anything."

"That's what I was afraid of."

Drew laughed and kept laughing until Cassie couldn't help joining in.

"All right," he said at last. "Forget everything I said about tonight. Never let it be said I dragged a fearful woman into my bed."

Cassie felt a pang of disappointment and then cursed herself for feeling it. He'd called her bluff, hadn't he? She'd acted suspicious of his motives, played coy, and now she'd have to make the first move. Drew wasn't reacting at all like the other men she'd known, but then why should he? He *was* different.

"Cassie?"

She glanced at him.

"That is the way you want it, right?"

"Yes," she lied.

"Then it's settled. If we're not too tired, we'll fly back today. If we are, we'll rent two rooms." He said it casually, as if the matter were of no importance to him.

"Okay." Why did she feel so bereft? Damn her insecurities!

"I'm going to take the controls back for a little bit. Are you game for a few stunts?"

"I...sure."

"Here goes. Don't close your eyes and take deep breaths."

Cassie did as she was told while the line of the horizon tilted and spun around once, then again and again. She gasped as the nose of the Cessna shot up toward the sky and over. When the plane began heading straight for the ground, she bit her tongue to keep from yelling at him to be careful. He had said she could trust him. Then Drew pulled the plane out of the dive, and they flew straight ahead once more.

Reaction quivered through her, and she sagged against the seat. But the excitement left her feeling more alive than ever before in her life. "Let's do that again," she said above the engine's din.

Drew glanced at her and caught his breath, knowing instinctively that after making love she would look exactly as she did right now. Why in the hell had he promised her two rooms tonight? He gripped the wheel and flipped the plane over once, twice, three times as his body pounded with increasing desire. He sent the nose downward in a spiral, and she cried out as they spun around and around.

As he flattened the spiral and brought the nose up, he heard her sigh. The sound carried a richness of emotion, a whisper of near fulfillment that left him aching. Yes. She would be this way in his arms, gasping and crying out for his touch, sighing as he came to her. Dammit, would she keep him away? Would she deny them both?

He turned his head and caught her watching him with an intensity he'd never seen before. His gaze traveled from her flushed face to the faint sheen of moisture on the exposed skin above the V of her blouse. Her chest rose and fell in rapid, shallow breaths, and her nipples thrust forward as taut as pencil erasers. She didn't speak, and neither did he. Reluctantly he brought his attention back to the horizon.

A.W.'S TINY MG HELD two people in relative comfort and three in complete discomfort. Cassie had to pretend she wasn't sitting in the lap of the man she'd been fantasizing about for the past two hours. Drew had to pretend Cassie was a gunnysack full of potatoes.

"Thought we'd go to The Golden Eagle for lunch, Drew," A.W. announced. "Ever been there, Cassie?"

"I've never been to Phoenix," Cassie shouted above the wind whipping through the convertible. Her hair would be a tangled mess when they arrived at the restaurant, but that was the least of her worries. She gripped the dashboard and tried to lean away from Drew's muscled chest. A.W. drove the little sportster as if they were at the bumper-car concession in an amusement park.

As they flew around corners and accelerated through amber lights, Cassie was thrown unceremoniously against Drew's hard body. The jolting contact buffeted her emotions far more than the wind played havoc with her hairdo.

In desperation she concentrated on the dapper man behind the wheel of the MG. A red touring cap sat jauntily on his head of gray hair. His dark aviator glasses were the kind she might have expected Drew to have on today. Except that he hadn't worn dark glasses.

Immediately Cassie's thoughts returned to Drew, to the plane flight and the passionate moment they'd shared. No, he hadn't worn dark glasses. If he had, she wouldn't have been able to see the expression in his eyes. Drew didn't try to hide anything. He was the most forthright man she'd ever met.

"When did you get the MG, Gramps?" Drew asked in a loud voice.

"A few months ago."

"Looks like it could use a little bodywork and a paint job."

"Yep. I thought it would be fun to fix up an older car. Besides, the Caddy was too clumsy. I wanted a little buggy that could move."

"It does that," Cassie agreed as another sharp turn crushed her against Drew.

"You smell good," he murmured before she disentangled herself and tried to sit up straighter.

So did he, Cassie admitted to herself. And felt good. For a moment his beard had tickled her ear, reminding her of how the soft hair had brushed her skin when he had kissed her the night of their racquetball match.

Desire squirmed within her, struggling to break through her self-imposed restraint. She could be in this man's arms tonight. It was her choice. "Where's The Golden Eagle?" she asked, more to distract herself than because she wanted to know.

"On top of the Valley Bank Center," A.W. said. "I like sitting above all that money."

"You'll enjoy the bird's-eye view," Drew commented, his voice rumbling from his chest and surrounding her, "considering the way you took to flying. I bet you're a sucker for the Tramway, too."

"You guessed it."

"Is that because you like being up high for a change?" he teased.

Before she could sputter an indignant retort, A.W. leaped gallantly to her rescue.

"Don't you dare call her short, Drew. She's petite. And better-looking than you deserve, with your smart mouth."

Cassie smiled. "Thank you, Dr. Bennett."

"A.W., please. And here we are." He stopped on a dime. "You two get out. I'll park this baby somewhere close and be back in a jiffy."

Drew and Cassie tumbled awkwardly out of the car and stepped to the sidewalk. Cassie smoothed her white poplin skirt and watched A.W. veer back into the flow of traffic whizzing by on the busy downtown street.

"He drives that thing like a bat out of hell," Drew remarked.

"I feel like one of twenty-five clowns that just piled out of the Volkswagen in the circus ring."

"Sorry about that. Last time I came over, he had a huge Cadillac. You could have packed the Los Angeles Rams into it."

"He likes to travel in style, doesn't he?"

"Always." Drew chuckled. "He's fun to be around."

"So's Grammy Jo."

They looked at each other solemnly.

Drew held out his hands, palms up. "See?"

"Yes. You're right. Now how do we get them together?"

"Leave that to me. He hasn't visited me in more than a year. He's about due."

"Okay, so we get him to Albuquerque. We can't just introduce them at that point. They're both too smart for that. They'd suspect immediately that we were match-making."

"I'll figure something out. Here he comes, so act like you're discussing something else."

"Okay. Have you always had that beard and mustache?" Cassie glanced up at him and batted her eyelashes.

"Huh? Oh, uh, yeah. I mean, no. I grew them after my divorce. Don't you like them?" He watched her dimples flash and knew she was teasing him. Well, that was okay. She could tease him until the cows came home if only she'd—Nope, he'd better forget that topic for now.

A.W. smiled broadly as he approached them. "Drew, you look damn good with a short woman. Makes you seem a bit more humble when you have to stoop a little to hear what she's saying."

Drew straightened immediately. Had he been leaning toward Cassie so obviously in the middle of this milling mass of humanity? He realized he hadn't noticed any of the crowd passing by. He, an inveterate people watcher, couldn't tear his attention away from a dimpled smile and a tousled mop of strawberry-blond hair. Cassie Larue had him hypnotized.

"Let's go, Gramps." Drew took Cassie's elbow and threw his other arm affectionately around the older man's shoulders. "I'm starved." The statement was true enough, although Drew wasn't referring to his lack of food.

After the waiter had seated them next to a window overlooking downtown Phoenix and they'd all exclaimed over the view, Cassie excused herself to rearrange her wind-damaged hair.

Sipping on the lemon-flavored water left by the bus-boy, Drew watched Cassie until she was out of sight.

A.W. folded his menu and laid it aside. "She's a real looker, but I guess I don't have to tell you that."

"I wanted you to meet her, Gramps."

"Did you, now? I don't remember you bringing any of your girlfriends around since Mavis. Is that right, or am I getting senile?"

Drew chuckled and shook his head. "That'll be the day. And you're right. This is the first woman I've wanted to drag over here for your approval in a long time. The funny thing is, I barely know her. I'm worried, Gramps."

"Why be worried? Enjoy it."

"Enjoy it? I feel like I've been invaded. She seems to understand me, can almost read my mind, and yet we've been on one date. She's wormed her way past my defenses, and I'm vulnerable as hell."

"That's not so bad. How'd you meet her?"

"She delivers my mail."

"That's different."

"Yeah." Drew rolled his water glass between his palms. "So how about you, Gramps? How's your love life?"

"Dull, my boy. Damn dull. One of the ladies I see wants to stuff me with fattening food. Another loves to sit around playing cards all day, and a third is bugging me to take up shuffleboard."

"You've only got three going? A few months ago I thought there were five."

"I'm paring down."

"Getting old, Gramps?" Drew teased.

"No, *they* are. They think old. I'd start in with a few

younger ones, except none of them can waltz worth a plugged nickel. I've tried the disco stuff, but what good is dancing if you can't rub up against each other a little?"

"Beats me." Drew smiled with satisfaction. He'd bet good money that Grammy Jo could waltz A.W.'s socks off. They were perfect for each other, and if they became involved, Cassie wouldn't have any excuses left. Snuggly little Cassie, who at this moment was wending her way through the crowded restaurant toward him.

Did she really stand out from everyone else, as if a spotlight followed her around? Probably not. She caught his gaze and smiled. Oh, God, he was a goner.

4

ALL DURING LUNCH Cassie wished her grandmother were with them, laughing and joking, filling out the foursome. She could hardly wait to bring the two spunky senior citizens—how they both hated that term—together. But she and Drew would have to be clever about the meeting. If either Grammy Jo or A.W. suspected they'd been set up, the entire scheme could fall through.

Drew and A.W. engaged in the usual male contest to see who would pay the bill, but Cassie could see the argument was a formality. A.W. wouldn't consider letting his grandson buy the meal. When the older man signed the credit-card slip, Cassie glanced at the signature out of habit.

The final *t* was crossed above the stem, as she would have expected from someone with a lifetime of high goals. The rest of the signature was almost impossible to read, a typical doctor's handwriting. Oh, well. Did she really need to see a sample of his handwriting to know that this man was the one for Grammy Jo? Everything about him was right. Her grandmother would even enjoy his maniacal style of driving. Cassie shuddered as she realized they'd soon be back in the little MG on the way to the Arizona State University campus and Drew's meeting.

"Sorry about this exterminating business, you two,"

A.W. apologized as he cut between a bus and a dump truck on the way to ASU. "You're sure Evan can get you back to the airport all right?"

"No problem, Gramps," Drew assured him.

From her position on Drew's lap, Cassie heard his muffled chuckle. Riding with Evan would be a breeze after what A.W. had put them through.

"That's good, because I'm expected in Wickenburg for cocktails."

"A woman?" Drew asked.

"Probably. I'm supposed to be visiting a couple your grandmother and I knew years ago, but I'm sure they'll have some poor widow invited to dinner. People are always trying to fix me up. Usually with dogs." A.W. whirled through the campus entrance and screeched to a stop in front of the red brick psych building, where groups of students in shorts and T-shirts lounged, waiting for the next class.

Drew and Cassie exchanged a glance. Yes, everyone was trying to fix up A.W., including them.

"End of the line," A.W. warbled, shifting the car into Neutral. "I've enjoyed meeting you, Cassie. Make Drew bring you back to Phoenix soon."

"We were talking about having you visit Albuquerque," Cassie said, deciding not to be deterred by A.W.'s aversion to matchmaking. Grammy Jo was not a dog. "He mentioned that you hadn't been there for quite a while."

"True, true. Just might do that, my boy."

"The Balloon Fiesta's in two weeks, Gramps. Didn't you say you wanted to ride in a hot-air balloon some day?"

"Absolutely. Two weeks, is it? Maybe I'll just drive over and experience that."

"Uh, Gramps, I'll be glad to fly over and pick you up."

"Nonsense. Time for me to get this little hummer out on the interstate and see what she can do."

Cassie groaned inwardly. Would A.W. kill himself on the way to his destiny with Grammy Jo? "But Drew's plane is so much faster," she urged.

"Not necessarily," A.W. replied and laughed uproariously at his own joke.

Cassie glanced in despair at Drew, who shrugged and rolled his eyes. A.W. would do what he wanted to. They'd have to keep their fingers crossed that he survived whatever adventures he undertook.

"Then we'll see you in two weeks," Drew confirmed as he and Cassie unfolded themselves once more from the car. "Take care, Gramps."

"Have you ever known me to be anything but careful?"

"Yes."

"That's how I stay young, my boy." With a quick salute he swerved the MG in a U-turn and sped off down the street.

"Whew." Cassie fumbled with the pins holding her hair on top of her head. "Doesn't he ever get speeding tickets?"

"Sure. He writes them off on his income tax as entertainment."

"I think Grammy Jo's met her match."

"Don't be so sure it won't be the other way around. I can picture A.W. doing aerobics in no time."

"I can hardly wait to see what happens when they

meet. Two weeks is fourteen days too long." Cassie pinned up a loose strand of hair.

"I know, but I had to come up with a plausible reason for him to visit. The balloon thing popped into my mind. He's always talked about taking one of those flights."

"So has Grammy Jo. In fact, if we play our cards right, we might have them sailing away in the same balloon before the visit's over. Good idea, Drew."

"I have them once in a while. Here, you missed a lock on the other side." He reached for the satiny curl and rubbed it between his fingers. "It's so soft, no wonder it doesn't stay. Give me one of those pins."

Cassie handed him a hairpin and stood perfectly still while he worked the loose strand in with the others. His fingers touched her scalp gently, sending little volts of excitement down her spine. Carefully he inserted the pin, tucked in another errant curl and moved back to survey his handiwork. Cassie sighed with disappointment that the task was over.

"What was that for?" He gave her a puzzled smile.

"I, um..." She opted for the truth. "That felt nice, having you fool with my hair. When I was a teenager, we used to mess with each other's hair all the time, and I always like it."

He stepped closer and cupped her face with his hands. "You're irresistible, you know that?"

"I'm not trying to be."

"That's why you are." He traced her cheekbones with his thumbs. "I can't seem to think of anything but kissing you, loving the hell out of you."

"You...you have a meeting," she said breathlessly.

"I know, dammit. I was going to suggest you take a

walk around the campus and come back here in an
hour or so, but I really don't want you to leave."

"But I'm going to." She stepped away from his
touch. "See you in an hour."

"I'll be in Evan Farber's office, third floor, second
door on the left."

"Fine." She waved and walked away. Without looking she knew he was standing there on the sidewalk
watching her until she was out of sight. It was a nice
sensation.

AN HOUR LATER she returned from her stroll around
the campus, where palm trees waved like giant feather
dusters in the warm desert breeze and students wore
as little clothing as their professors would allow. Their
seemingly carefree attitude and cheerful banter made
Cassie feel considerably older, although she'd been
part of such a life only five years ago.

Everywhere she looked, the mating game was in
progress. What had Drew said about the field narrow-
ing after high school and college? He was right. The
halls of education were teeming with prospective part-
ners in ways that the everyday work world was not.
Even so, she'd been handed the gift of Drew. Was she
going to louse that up with her reluctant attitude?

Determined to renegotiate their arrangement for tonight, Cassie climbed the concrete stairway to the third
floor and located Evan's office. She tapped lightly on
the door.

"Come in," Drew called. "We're about finished," he
continued as she walked through the doorway. "I'd
like you to meet Evan Farber. Evan, this is Cassie Larue."

Evan stood behind his desk and held out his hand. "Drew mentioned you flew over with him. I'm delighted to meet you, Cassie."

Cassie accepted his firm handshake and decided she'd probably like Evan Farber. The walls of his office were hung with bright skiing posters, and his welcoming smile was equally cheerful. His hair was thinning on top, and as if to compensate, he wore it down to his collar in back. With his wire-rimmed glasses, he looked like a modern Ben Franklin.

"Well, Ev," Drew said as he rose from his chair, "I don't think I've been of much help. It's tough trying to evaluate someone who's not fluent in English."

"I know. Spanish would have been easier to deal with, but Portuguese?"

Cassie glanced at Evan. "One of your clients speaks Portuguese?"

"Unfortunately. He knows a little English, but not enough to take the standard psychological tests I've been trying to give him."

"Has he written anything for you?" Cassie asked without thinking.

"No. But I'm sure he writes in Portuguese. I could have it translated, but—"

"You wouldn't have to translate it," she said, eager to help this friendly-looking man. "I could analyze the writing as is."

"Analyze it? What do you mean?" Evan asked.

And then Cassie realized that she'd just revealed the secret she'd been keeping from Drew. And a clumsy revelation it was, at that. One glance at his face told her he wasn't pleased. But the damage was done, and Evan was waiting for an answer.

"I'm a certified graphoanalyst. I analyze people's handwriting."

"That's fascinating. Did you know that, Drew?"

"Nope."

The single word of denial spoke eloquently of Drew's disapproval. Cassie glanced nervously in his direction and found him studying her closely. She was in for some tough questioning after this meeting was over.

Evan looked from Drew to Cassie, obviously aware of the sudden tension in the room. "Well, Cassie," he said at last, "I'd be delighted with any insight you can provide. I'll have this fellow write something, and I'll mail it to you in the next day or so, if you'll give me your address."

"Of course." Cassie scribbled her name and Grammy Jo's address on a notepad Evan pushed forward.

He reached into a holder on his desk, pulled out a business card and handed it to her. "Keep in touch. I'll be interested in your interpretation. I've been following this stuff— What do you call it?"

"Graphoanalysis."

"Right. Anyway, some of my colleagues consider it hocus-pocus." Evan paused to allow Drew to comment, but his friend remained silent. "I don't think so. Makes sense to me that a person's writing would reflect certain attitudes. After all, none of us writes exactly alike, do we?"

"No, we don't." Cassie could feel Drew's hostility radiating toward her. He was one of the psychologists who labeled the study of handwriting hocus-pocus, she was sure.

"I think Cassie and I had better be going," Drew said gruffly. "Are you still free to take us to the airport, Evan?"

"My chariot awaits in the parking lot." He stacked the papers on his desk and ushered them out of the office.

On the ride to the airport, Cassie made stilted conversation, but she couldn't relax, knowing that a confrontation with Drew was close at hand. He believed in openness, she'd learned that from his handwriting. She hadn't been open with him, not completely.

"Where shall I drop you?" Evan asked as they neared the airport.

"The executive terminal is fine."

Cassie realized that Drew's answer meant they were going home. Well, what did she expect? An angry man didn't suggest a night of fun and games with the person who had made him angry.

Evan parked the car and got out to shake Drew's hand. "Thanks for the consultation. Let me know when I can return the favor."

"Glad to do it, Evan."

"And I'll get that handwriting sample, Cassie."

"Fine." Cassie shook Evan's hand and smiled, a little sad to leave a promising ally for what she knew would be a full-scale argument.

When Evan drove away, she turned to the tall man beside her. "I'm sorry I didn't tell you about this before."

"So am I."

"You're probably ready to forget everything, including the matchup between A.W. and Grammy Jo."

"It crossed my mind."

"Well, I can't blame you, but I wish you'd reconsider that part, at least. What happens between us isn't important, but I'd hate for those two people to miss out because we had a parting of the ways."

"What the hell do you mean? What happens between us is very important! A.W. and Grammy Jo are secondary, as far as I'm concerned. Look, I'd rather not stand out here and discuss this."

"Let's just get in the plane and fly home, Drew." Cassie started toward the terminal.

"No." He grabbed her arm.

"I thought you didn't want to discuss anything out here."

He grasped her other arm and brought her close to him. "You know what I want? I want to stop playing games. I want to get our suitcases out of that plane, take a shuttle bus to the nearest hotel, rent one damn room and cut the crap!"

"But—"

"But nothing! You've spent weeks analyzing my handwriting, haven't you?"

"Yes."

"Then you must know me pretty damn well by now if you believe that stuff, right?"

She lifted her chin. "Yes, I believe 'that stuff,' as you call it, and yes, I know you very well."

"Then you have the advantage, lady, because I didn't know nearly that much about you, and yet I was willing to take a chance. I was sticking my neck out, revealing exactly how I felt about you, ignorant as hell, vulnerable as hell. And you sat there with all kinds of information about me and played hard to get. Is that fair?"

"Maybe not."

"Maybe? I'm tired of taking all the risks here. I'm ready for you to invest a little of yourself and even things up."

Cassie began to quiver in his grasp. He was right. God, he was absolutely right. In her mania to protect herself, she'd let him take all the chances. Now it was her turn to roll the dice for a change. Her voice was hoarse when she finally was able to answer him. "Let's get the suitcases."

Without a word he released her, and they walked together through the terminal and out to the plane. After retrieving their luggage, he arranged for a shuttle to take them to a hotel.

Throughout the process Cassie took furtive peeks at Drew's face, but his lips were still set in a grim line. The softness and caring she was used to were gone from his gaze.

"One question, Cassie." He paused after they'd entered the lobby. "Should I make a stop at the hotel's drug counter?"

Cassie flushed, but she wasn't really surprised by Drew's question. A man with his sense of responsibility would make certain about birth control, no matter how intense his emotions became. "No," she replied in a low voice. "I take... It's okay."

"Good." Drew returned to his silence as they registered and took an elevator up to the room.

The decor was generic, and Cassie wouldn't have been able to describe even the color scheme. Her entire focus was on the bearded man who flung their suitcases on the floor and unhooked the Do Not Disturb sign from the doorknob.

He hung the sign on the outside of the door, locked it and strode over to the king-sized bed. After tossing the covers aside, he turned to her. When he spoke, his voice was softer than she'd expected.

"Now," he said.

Cassie thought her heart would pound itself out of her chest as he came toward her, his dark eyes ablaze. She swallowed convulsively.

"Are you really so afraid of me?" A hint of his former gentleness tinged his voice.

She shook her head.

"I won't hurt you, Cassie. But I don't want you to hurt me, either." He lifted his hands to her hair and began working the pins out one by one, tossing them carelessly to the carpet. When all the soft strands tumbled free, he combed through them with both hands until the tangles were gone. Slowly he massaged her scalp with the tips of his fingers until her eyes closed and her head lolled back against his supporting palms.

His lips touched her throat, her chin, her closed eyelids and at last her mouth. With a muffled groan he gripped her head more tightly and parted her lips with deliberate pressure.

The silken caress of his mustache, the sensual brush of his beard against her skin firmly imprinted his identity. This was not just any man kissing her; this was Drew. Drew of the bold handwriting, the decisive manner, the inquisitive mind.

Blindly she reached for him, clutching his shoulders for balance as her world spun in ever tighter circles. His mouth moved ravenously against hers, and she dug her fingers into the muscles of his upper arms in reaction to the onslaught of emotions he provoked. She couldn't think, couldn't move, couldn't imagine anything beyond this melding of his mouth with hers as he demanded the surrender she gave because she could do no less.

He had kissed her before, but not like this. The first time he had explored; now he claimed possession. The desire that had smoldered between them all day fueled the response of their heated bodies, and when at last he released her, they stood staring at each other, their breath coming in gasps.

"My God, Cassie."

A smile trembled on her lips. "Who's afraid now?" she whispered.

"I am." Slowly he began unbuttoning his shirt. "But I wouldn't miss this for the world."

"Neither would I." Cassie kept her gaze on him while she stepped out of her shoes and unfastened her skirt.

He pulled off his shirt, displaying shoulders wide and muscled from his weight lifting. A triangle of curling hair matted his broad chest. Cassie longed for the abrasion of that dark hair against her breasts.

Deliberately he kept going, taking off shoes, socks, slacks and finally the last barrier to her hungry eyes. He was beautifully made, and the sight of him, erect and bold, sent a rush of warm moisture between her thighs.

With clumsy fingers she removed her blouse, and his gaze followed her progress. Tossing the blouse aside, she arched her back and unhooked her bra. Slowly she let it slide down her arms to the floor and waited, heart pounding, for Drew's reaction.

The reaction proved to be hers. Without physically

touching her, he caressed her so thoroughly with a glance that her breasts tightened and throbbed in response. Instinctively she cradled the tender weight in both palms, but her skin burned with a fire only he could extinguish.

Uttering a sound low in his throat, he moved toward her. Sure hands found the waistband of her lace panties and ripped them away with one quick twist. Then he stepped back and traced every curve with his gaze, pausing at each pouting nipple and at the dark blond curls that covered the treasure he sought.

In one motion he scooped her up and placed her on the cool sheets. For a moment he stood above her, trembling with anticipation and fighting for control. He hadn't meant to rip her underwear from her body. If he took this too fast, he wouldn't learn all that he wanted to know about her.

He wanted to discover what made her cry out, as she had today in the plane, what made her whimper with delight, what made her crazy with lust. He wanted to unearth the elemental part of her that responded to those rough-and-tumble moments high in the air, close to the sun. Then he would know her.

Her hazel eyes were luminous as he lowered his body next to hers. Her hair tumbled over the white pillowcase with the same abandon he wanted to bring to the rest of her. But his own body clamored for release, and the kiss he'd meant to be light and teasing turned into something else when her soft hands molded the planes of his chest and moved lower to stroke his swollen manhood.

He hadn't thought she'd be so daring, and what little restraint he had deserted him. With a moan of capitulation, he moved over her. With his first thrust he murmured in recognition, as if he'd known how she would wrap him about with liquid warmth, how the pulse of her body would tune to his, how her panting breath would sound against his ear.

He had meant this first time to be a soft, sweet melody, a slow crescendo, a chance to learn. But her body was a wild thing, urging him on with undulating movements of her hips and gasping whispers of need.

She called his name, and he felt her tighten around him. As delirium took him in its powerful grip and his own response rushed forward, he heard her cry out and knew it was the sound he had to hear, the sound that told him she was giving him a glimpse of her soul.

THE ROOM WAS ALMOST DARK when Cassie awoke. Drew was still half slumped over her. She was amazed that they'd both fallen asleep so easily, so naturally. So trustingly.

She'd never gone to sleep after making love to a man before, but then she'd never made love to anyone like Drew. His honest approach eliminated any pretending, any shyness, any of the awkward emotions couples usually feel the first time they lie in each other's arms.

With Drew the experience had been explosive, overwhelming. He had wanted her to invest something in this relationship, and she felt as if she'd just plunked down her life savings.

Cassie shifted her weight, and Drew stirred against her. Gradually he awoke, then smiled sleepily in the dim light. "Guess I dozed off."

"Me, too. I've never done that before, Drew."

"I'm glad you did this time. Otherwise, you'd think I was a real dully guy, falling asleep on you like that. The accepted behavior is to talk afterward, reassure each other about the fine time we both had."

Cassie chuckled.

"Does that giggle mean you didn't need reassurance?"

"Something like that."

"God, neither did I. I've never been more reassured in my life. Cassie..."

"What?"

He rolled his weight from her but kept one arm securely around her waist, holding her close. "I'm sorry if I sounded a little harsh back at the terminal."

"I deserved it. I was doing just what you said—holding myself aloof and allowing you to reveal everything about yourself first."

Drew propped his head in his hand. "I think the aloof is gone," he murmured, cupping one breast and stroking the tip with his thumb.

"Yes," she said with a ragged sigh, "I think you're right."

"But we missed a few steps along the way." He traced a path to her other breast and circled the aureole with the tip of his finger until her nipple tightened to a firm nub.

A languorous warmth suffused Cassie's body. "Did we? I didn't notice."

"Well, we did," he said, bending to kiss the hollow of her throat. "And I'm going to remedy that right now."

Cassie welcomed the remedy as she discovered the special delights of being kissed all over by a bearded man. As his tongue and lips paid moist homage to each swollen breast, his soft hair whispered over her skin, brushing it to a tingling awareness she'd never known before.

He was relentlessly thorough, moving from the valley between her breasts to her flat stomach and below, until she moaned his name aloud and begged him to fill her again with his throbbing strength.

With maddening slowness he retraced his path while she writhed under him. At last he reached her lips once more, and she grasped his hips to guide him to her.

"Wait," he said, breathing hard. He groped for the bedside lamp and turned it on.

Cassie blinked as the light washed over them.

"I want to watch your face," he murmured, kissing her forehead and her cheeks. "You're all warm and flushed, and you smell wonderful. I want to feast all my senses on you, Cassie."

She met his heated gaze and knew that she wanted to see his face, too. "Love me, Drew," she whispered.

She drew in her breath as he eased into her with exquisite tenderness. He closed his eyes for a moment when they were locked together as closely as they could possibly be. Then he gazed down at her, wonder in his dark eyes.

Cassie answered with a tremulous smile.

"You're a miracle, Cassie."

"No."

"Yes." He moved within her, watching the passion deepen in her eyes, the breath come ever faster through her parted lips.

Cassie drank in the fierce emotion she saw etched on

Drew's face. His intense involvement fed her own excitement. She murmured to him—first words and then only primitive sounds, building at last to an abandoned cry of fulfillment that blended with his own shout of joy.

His image wavered as the convulsions rocked her, and then her view of him steadied once more.

He gulped in great amounts of air, and his chest heaved, but he kept his gaze fixed on her. "Yes," he managed to say at last. "That's what I wanted to see. The same kind of raw feeling you had up in the plane today. God, you're magnificent, Cassie."

"So are you."

"I'll have to be, to keep up with you." He smiled and smoothed her tousled hair. "We started this program in the middle of the day. We've got a whole night together before we fly home tomorrow."

Cassie wiggled under him. **"Good."**

"Uh-huh." He kissed her gently. "I don't want to starve you, though. It must be past dinnertime. Why don't we head down to the dining room? I bet you brought something nice to wear for dinner, and I ought to give you a chance to model it."

Cassie laughed, thinking of her red eyelet sundress. At this point the garment seemed like overkill. "I also brought a nightgown," she said.

"Let's not get carried away," Drew said, tweaking her nose.

They showered and dressed together, and Drew admired the way the red eyelet teased but revealed nothing. At dinner he kept glancing at her bodice and whispering bawdy suggestions until both of them wondered if they could finish the main course without rushing back to the room and throwing themselves into each other's arms.

"We've paid for this food, so we might as well eat it," Cassie said, cutting into her veal.

"You're far too practical. Anyway, haven't you ever heard of doggy bags?"

"I don't think a doggy bag would work for veal Parmesan."

"Then eat fast. I want to untie those laces and—"

"Stop it, Drew. Let's change the subject."

"I can't."

"Then I will. Do you think Evan will get that handwriting sample for me?"

"Probably. That's quite a hobby you have, Cassie. Threw me for a loop, but I guess it's harmless enough."

Cassie had been about to take a bite, but at Drew's words she laid the forkful of food back on the plate and stared at him. "Graphoanalysis is not a hobby for me, Drew."

"What else would you call it? The process is about in the same class as fortune-telling, isn't it?"

"A lot of people have that misconception." She gripped her wineglass, as if by grasping it tightly she would hold on to her temper. "Maybe because libraries used to have books on handwriting stuck in with material on the occult."

Drew's smile was teasing. "Are you a witch, Cassie?"

"Graphoanalysis isn't witchcraft." She looked directly at him. "In fact, the Library of Congress has changed the classification from occult to individual psychology."

"Psychology? Listen, Cassie, I'm a psychologist. I've

trained for years to learn how to decipher people's personalities. I have trouble believing that reading a book about upstrokes and downstrokes and how someone dots his *i*'s can be called psychology."

"I did more than read a book, Drew. I've taken an entire course of study; it took me a solid year. I'm certified by the International Graphoanalysis Society."

Drew snorted. "Sounds like another diploma mill to me."

Cassie began to tremble with hurt and rage. She'd encountered this sort of prejudice before. Usually she ignored the naysayers, but this time the derision was coming from a source she couldn't ignore.

She wasn't sure when it had happened, when her attraction to this man had changed to something more. But sometime during the long, eventful day they'd shared, she'd fallen in love with Drew Bennett.

5

CASSIE FOLDED HER NAPKIN. "May I have the key? I'd like to go back to the room."

"I'll go with you," Drew said immediately, pushing back his chair.

"I'd rather you didn't." She stood.

"What?" He stared at her in disbelief.

"I'd like some time alone."

"Do you mean to tell me that you're stomping away because I don't share your views of this handwriting business?"

"I'm tired of talking about it, that's all."

"You're angry."

"Brilliant deduction, Mr. Psychologist. Or I should say Dr. Psychologist, shouldn't I? I haven't been using your title all this time. With those long years of training, I'm sure you expect proper deference when you're addressed."

Drew rose. "Cut it out, Cassie. Sarcasm doesn't become you."

"How about bootlicking? Would you prefer that?"

"Cassie..."

She held out her hand. "The key, please."

He glared at her a moment longer before reaching into his pant pocket and extracting the key. He placed it in her palm and turned toward the bar. "Don't wait up for me."

"I wouldn't dream of it." Cassie stalked away, determined to reach the elevator before the tears started. Once in the room she let them flow in torrents amid a string of angry curses. How dared he ruin what they had found together with his arrogant attitude? How dared he be her wonderful prince, only to turn into a croaking frog? Damn him. Damn him to hell.

She paced the small area, crying and swearing. She thought of all the things she might have said to convince him about the legitimacy of graphoanalysis. His reaction had wounded her so much that she had abandoned logical arguments. She wanted to hurt him as he'd hurt her.

Two hours later, Cassie was still awake, the tension of all that had happened to her that day keeping her eyes wide open in the darkness. She'd donned her modest nightgown, washed her face and brushed her teeth, all tiny rituals that should have soothed her toward sleep.

Had she been wrong to leave the dining room so abruptly? Perhaps if she and Drew could have a calm discussion about the study of handwriting, he would change his opinion. Except he was in the bar, possibly getting blitzed. Cassie didn't want to search him out down there. And he might be beyond discussion.

So she waited, wondering if and when he'd return. He wouldn't strand her at the hotel, would he? Certainly not with his own suitcase still in the room. No, that wasn't in his character. He'd see that she got home, and Cassie would have another chance to determine if they could rationally handle the subject of handwriting.

When his knock finally sounded at the door, she switched on a light and got out of bed. "Who is it?" she asked automatically, although she was sure it was Drew.

"I gave you my key," came the muffled response, "and I can't get in."

She squelched the rebellious temptation to leave him out there. That wouldn't solve anything, but it might salve her battered ego. No, they needed to talk. That is, if he was in any shape to talk after all that time in the bar.

She opened the door and stood silently while he walked past her. He smelled faintly of bourbon and cigarette smoke, and he looked tired.

"Sorry to get you out of bed," he said, glancing at her nightgown. "Cassie—"

"Drew, I was a little quick on the trigger tonight. I'd like to think we can both be more adult about this disagreement."

"So would I." He rubbed the back of his neck. "But damned if I can think straight after three strong drinks and all that's gone on today." Slowly he began removing his clothes. "How about we sleep on it?"

"Okay." Cassie crossed to the bed and slid under the covers. "I'm pretty tired, too." At least she should be, she thought. But could she fall peacefully asleep next to this disturbing, infuriating, yet very sexy man?

She lay curled in a ball and listened to water splashing in the bathroom sink. Damn him, he still had the power to excite her, in spite of his pigheadedness. But she vowed to control her physical attraction.

He crawled into bed, and she switched off the light. When he circled her waist with one arm and pulled her toward him, her anger flared, and she resisted. Now that they were in bed, he behaved as if nothing were wrong between them!

"Come on, Cassie. Don't let this ruin what we have." He cupped one of her breasts and gently stroked the nipple. "Let me love you."

She rolled to face him, her body tense with the effort of ignoring his touch. "I won't put my feelings in compartments like that, Drew. I'd feel like a hypocrite, falling right into your arms after we've just had a fight."

"Haven't you heard? That's how people make up." He stroked her hair back from her face. "And I don't know about you, but I'm not angry anymore."

"Well, I am. And furthermore, I think we have some things to discuss before we—"

"Oh, Cassie." His sigh whispered over her face. "Can't we discuss in the morning? Tonight I want to feel your softness under me. I've been sitting in the bar thinking about how stupid it was for me to be down there and you to be up here, when we could be together." He caressed her hip through the soft nightgown. "We're so damn good together. Let's not waste this time."

"I'm sorry, Drew." Somehow she found the strength of will to turn away from him. How easy it would have been to give in and let the lovemaking happen. But their unsettled argument would have taken so much away from the complete joy she had felt that afternoon. "In the morning we'll talk and then see how things are," she finished vaguely.

For a while he didn't say anything. Then with a muttered "Damn," he rolled to his side of the bed.

Cassie listened to him breathe and wondered if either of them would be able to sleep tonight. Eventually she fell into a restless slumber, but she awoke as soon as dawn filtered through the hotel's miniblinds.

Quietly she eased out of bed and headed for the bathroom. When she returned, Drew was awake and watching her.

"It's morning," he said, his voice husky with sleep as he propped a pillow behind his head. "Ready to talk? Or would you rather..." He allowed his voice to trail off as he lifted one eyebrow suggestively.

Cassie looked away from the appeal of his bare chest above the fold of white sheet. "I'd rather talk." She sat on the desk chair several feet away from the bed and straightened the shoulder straps of her nightgown.

"You can come over here." He patted the mattress next to him.

"I feel more comfortable like this."

He shrugged. "Suit yourself." He reached for her pillow and made himself a backrest before leaning back with arms folded. "Fire away."

"Didn't I read somewhere that folded arms mean someone doesn't want to listen?"

"Sometimes. Not always. But okay, I'll unfold my arms. You, I might point out, have your legs crossed."

She couldn't help but smile. "Guess I'd better be careful trading comments like that with a psychologist."

"That's right."

Cassie took a deep breath. "Drew, I wish I could change your opinion about graphoanalysis. I don't think you're giving the subject a fair chance."

"Cassie, do you realize how many quacks there are running around pretending they can delve into a person's psyche? I'm sorry, but handwriting experts seem to be popping up everywhere these days. I've been to parties where someone analyzes handwriting for the entertainment of the guests."

"Maybe that's not the best way to earn respectability, but I'll admit to having done that. Because I don't need complicated tests and I carry so much of what I know in my head, spot analysis is easy."

"I have a lot of knowledge in my head, too. But I don't use psychology as a party trick."

"What's wrong with dispensing knowledge informally? Does everything scholarly have to take place inside a clinic or something?"

"Not necessarily. But I would expect some dignity, at least."

"Drew Bennett, I think maybe you're a snob," she accused.

"Maybe."

"Did you know that many employers use handwriting analysis to screen prospective employees?"

"I'd heard of that, but I'd hate to think someone decided to hire me or not on the basis of my handwriting."

"Would you submit to a psychological evaluation?"

"Of course."

"Handwriting analysis is no different."

He leaned forward, and the pillows fell behind him with a soft plop. "The hell it isn't! Those tests are fairly accurate. Validity studies are done on them."

"Validity studies are done on handwriting traits, too."

"By whom?"

"The people at the institute in Chicago where I got my training."

"You went there?"

"Only for the annual congress. My course was through correspondence." She resented his disdainful expression. "I worked very hard for my certification! Not for as long as you did for a PhD, but I intend to keep taking courses. In fact, I expect to keep learning all my life."

"So do I," he said quietly.

"Then why not open your mind and learn about handwriting? It's another tool, Drew! Why can't you accept that?"

"I'm sorry, Cassie. I just can't. Not even to please you."

She became very still. "Then I guess our discussion is over."

"And obviously a few other things. Can't we agree to disagree on this?"

"No." She shook her head. "Not on this." She stood and reached for her suitcase. "I think we'd better get back to Albuquerque." Sick with regret for what couldn't be, she began preparing for the trip home.

His attitude had prevented her from telling him her dream—that eventually she would leave the mail-carrier job and become a full-time graphoanalyst. She'd already collected a few fees for her labors, and with the right connections someday she might be able to make a living in the work she loved.

Drew wouldn't understand her dream. In fact, he might laugh at it. Therefore, in spite of the strong physical attraction she felt for him, Cassie had to put a stop to what they had started. With a certain malicious intent she picked the moment when they were flying over the terrain where he'd done the stunts the day before to tell him of her decision.

"Drew, I believe it's best if we end our association," she said carefully but loudly enough that he would hear her clearly over the drone of the engine. Then she folded her hands in her lap so that he wouldn't see them shaking.

"I've felt that coming all morning." He sighed. "Why, Cassie?"

"I think you know why."

"And I think you're overreacting. We disagree about one small matter. Nobody agrees on everything, Cassie."

"In the first place, graphoanalysis is not a small matter, as far as I'm concerned. And in the second place, your disdain for it implies a certain disrespectful attitude toward me."

"You're taking this too personally."

"There's no other way to take it. I believe in what I'm doing. You act as if someone involved in this pursuit has a screw loose. If you don't have any more respect for my intelligence than that, why should we continue? Or do you enjoy bedding silly women?"

"Cassie, stop it!"

"We only have one small complication," she continued, trying to keep her voice from breaking. "We started out to bring two unusual older people together, and I still would like to do that."

"How noble of you."

"Obviously I can't go on with the plan without your cooperation."

"That's true. And by the way, what is the plan? I've

been a little, uh, distracted lately, but I don't recall that we made one."

"We didn't, but I have. It's not great, considering our circumstances, but it's all I can think of right now."

He sounded wary. "What do you have in mind?"

"If we pretend to A.W. and Grammy Jo that our relationship is flourishing, then a party to introduce me to all your friends would be appropriate. You can have it while A.W. is in Albuquerque, and naturally you would invite Grammy Jo to that sort of open house."

"But of course we'd only be pretending that our relationship is flourishing, right?" He stared straight ahead at the clear blue sky.

"That's right. After Grammy Jo and A.W. meet, whether our relationship is on or off will cease to be important."

"Oh, it will, will it? To whom?"

"To both of us, I assume."

"Cassie, you're an idiot."

"I figured that was your assessment."

"Dammit, woman! Can't you tell that I'm crazy about you? Don't let this handwriting thing assume so much importance between us."

"The importance was already there. You just refuse to recognize it, Drew. Consider how you'd feel if I said trying to rehabilitate prisoners through counseling was a waste of time."

The plane's engine throbbed in the silence. "You insist on equating my profession with your pastime, don't you?"

Her voice was brittle. "Yes, I do."

He didn't speak for several minutes, and then he sighed in resignation. "A party, huh?"

"If you agree."

"Why not? I'm certainly in the mood for one."

"Sarcasm doesn't become you."

"Sorry. I'm learning how to use it in self-defense."

She ignored his gibe. "When you find out exactly when A.W.'s arriving, we can plan the party for the first night he's in Albuquerque. That way he and Grammy Jo will have the maximum number of days to become acquainted."

"Wait a minute. He won't arrive for about two weeks, and yet you and I are supposed to be a hot number. Won't Grammy Jo be suspicious if I don't hang around a lot between now and then?"

"I've considered that, too."

"Naturally."

"I'll explain to Grammy Jo that you're snowed under with work on a special project with a two-week deadline. We've agreed to take some time off together when you're finished. If you'll call me several times, that will help. You can hang up right away, and I'll just pretend to have an extended conversation with you."

"Sounds like fun."

"Are you going to cooperate or not? Because if not, say so now before we go any further with this thing."

"Oh, I'll cooperate, Cassie, my love. You'll find me extremely cooperative."

My love. The words sliced through her, hurting more than she could have believed possible. Swallowing hard, she stared out the window at the tiny shadow of the plane sliding along the desert landscape toward Albuquerque.

GRAMMY JO WAS LEAFING THROUGH a copy of *Vogue* when Cassie walked into the house with her suitcase.

Her grandmother looked up from the magazine and smiled. "Have a nice time?"

"Wonderful," Cassie warbled, heading for her bedroom so that she didn't have to look Grammy Jo in the eye.

"Even with the old coot as a chaperone?"

"He's not an old coot," Cassie called from her bedroom. "He's very nice." She debated whether to say more, to speak in glowing terms of A.W. No, better not. She might arouse Grammy Jo's suspicions, especially because A.W. was going to show up in Albuquerque.

"What's his house like?"

"I don't know. We...we stayed in a hotel."

"Now *that* sounds better." Grammy Jo came to lean against the bedroom door frame. "But how come? I thought you were all set to stay at his house."

Cassie averted her face as she continued to unpack. "He was having an exterminator spray for crickets, and he left to spend the night with friends in Wickenburg. Drew and I were on our own."

"How delicious."

"Mmm."

"But spraying for crickets seems an unlikely story to me."

"That's what he said."

Grammy Jo chuckled. "Well, I doubt that was the real reason you three didn't sleep under the same roof. Anyway, I'm glad everything turned out well."

"Sure did," Cassie said, forcing a light tone.

"And I can see you don't want me prying into the intimate details. That's fine, sweetheart. And I'm really thrilled for you."

"Thanks, Grammy Jo." With great effort Cassie smiled at her grandmother.

"You don't look like you got much sleep, dear."

"No, and I think I'll take a nap."

Grammy Jo grinned indulgently. "You do that."

Cassie nodded. When her grandmother left to finish reading her magazine, she dropped to the bed and buried her head in her hands.

SOMEHOW CASSIE SURVIVED the first week of being without Drew, of delivering his mail without seeing him. They had agreed that he mustn't be home when she drove her route. She even considered putting in for a transfer, but she couldn't make herself do it. Painful though it was, she still treasured the chance to drive past his house every day.

Evan Farber's letter arrived with the sample of writing from his Portuguese client. Cassie analyzed it with great thoroughness, anxious to demonstrate her professionalism. She held on to the tiny hope that Evan might someday show her work to Drew, although she doubted anything would change Drew's mind about graphoanalysis.

During her hours at home, Cassie spent much of her time pretending to Grammy Jo how beautifully the love affair with Drew was progressing. But when it came to excitement over his frequent phone calls, Cassie discovered she didn't have to pretend. She lived for the sound of his voice, even as she cursed herself as a stupid fool for still being in love with him.

The plan for him to call several times and hang up

immediately hadn't worked out quite that way. He always had something to tell her, some funny story about a client, an experience with the plane or a comment on some item in the news. With the expertise of his profession, he involved her in conversations that often stretched for an hour or more.

"If he has that much time, why doesn't he come over?" Grammy Jo asked after one especially long phone call.

Cassie thought quickly. "Grammy Jo, if we got within ten feet of each other, we'd spend a lot more time than that, believe me." She winked. "After all, if Drew's flying that plane everywhere, he needs his sleep."

"So why not get moved in together and end the agony?"

"I, uh, we..."

"I've shocked my granddaughter."

Cassie grasped at the excuse for her fumbling. "I guess so."

"You're not staying here because of me, are you?"

"Of course not! The truth is, Drew hasn't mentioned having me stay with him."

"So?"

"So I'm old-fashioned enough to want him to be the one to broach the subject." There. Maybe that would satisfy her grandmother.

Grammy Jo mumbled something slightly off-color and said good-night, leaving Cassie to another miserable eight hours of tossing and turning and longing for Drew. She hoped to God he was suffering, too. But then she thought of the danger to him if he didn't get enough sleep, just as she'd mentioned to Grammy Jo, and she began to worry about that. What a mess!

When next he called, she had worked herself into a fit of concern about the possibility that he'd crash his plane because he wasn't well rested. She imagined a slight note of fatigue beneath his usual greeting.

"Drew, are you...are you getting enough sleep?"

He met her question with silence. As last he spoke. "Why, Cassie?"

"I...I just wondered. You're flying a lot, and I'm sure you can't afford to be tired when you're in the air."

"So?"

"So are you sleeping well?"

"No. Are you?"

"No."

"Cassie—"

"I think you should take something. There are some very good products on the market now, and—"

"You want me to replace you with drugs?"

It was the first personal conversation they'd had all week, and Cassie's heart began to beat frantically. As long as they discussed his work or some general topic, she was in pretty good shape. "Drew, you might as well get used to the situation," she said, her voice quavering.

"What if I can't?"

"You have to."

"I've tried, believe me, Cassie. But I'm going nuts, not being able to hold you, kiss you, make love—"

"Don't, Drew."

"Are you lying on your bed, Cassie?"

"No," she said, sitting up straight on the mattress.

"Remember what it was like, holding each other? I

can't forget the softness of your breasts, the warmth of—"

"Drew, I'm going to hang up."

"A.W.'s arriving Wednesday."

Cassie squeezed her eyes shut. "Oh."

"The party's at seven. Wear your red dress, Cassie."

"No."

"It's the sort of thing a woman in love would wear. Isn't that supposed to be the role you're playing?"

It's no role! Cassie wanted to scream. *I love you, and I wish to hell I didn't!* "Maybe I'll buy something new," she said. "Are there any colors you don't like?"

"I'm touched that you asked. Let's see. I'm not too fond of that sort of orangy-pink color. What's it called?"

"Peach."

"Yeah, peach."

"Good. I saw a peach dress in Goldwater's the other day. I think I'll get it."

"Cassie Larue, you little—"

"Careful, Drew. The phone company doesn't appreciate profanity on the lines."

"And you'd probably report me, wouldn't you?"

"Not until after Wednesday. I can hardly wait to get this over with."

"Is that right? I haven't noticed you rushing to hang up the phone when I call."

"You're marginally more interesting than television, that's all, and I haven't picked up any good books lately."

His voice was soft, almost as if he were smiling as he spoke. "Liar."

"Is A.W. driving over?"

"I'm afraid so."

"Then he'll have his little car to squire Grammy Jo around in—if he gets here. He's a terrible driver, Drew."

"I know it looks that way, but I watched carefully when we were in Phoenix. He's wild, but he knows exactly what he's doing. His reflexes are excellent. If I'd thought we were in danger, I wouldn't have let you get back in that car."

His caring flowed over her, a soothing balm for her raw emotions. "Drew, I—"

"Cassie, let me come over. Now. We'll have some coffee. Talk a little. I need to see you."

"No, Drew."

"Dammit, Cassie, this is ridiculous."

"You're right. Grammy Jo and I will be there on Wednesday, Drew. You needn't call again."

"That's four days."

"I'll fake something. Really, Drew, this is too painful. After Wednesday we can cut the ties completely, and everything will be easier."

"You don't believe that."

"Yes, I do." And she did. Nothing could be worse than what she was going through at that moment, hearing his voice on the other end of the telephone, remembering the sound of his whispers in her ear as they made love.

"Cassie, please let me see you. It's been so long, and I need—"

"No, Drew." She hung up the phone without saying goodbye. Grabbing a pillow from her bed, she hugged it against the unbearable ache inside her.

Across town, Drew replaced the receiver in its cradle

and looked at the stack of books on his bedside table. Before his call to Cassie, he'd gone to the library. Checking out the books on handwriting analysis hadn't been easy for him to do, and he hoped nobody he knew had seen him do it. With a grimace he opened the first one and began to read.

6

CASSIE BUTTONED the peach dress all the way up to her neck. Combs held her hair back on both sides, but it tumbled freely down her back, and her makeup was minimal. She looked exactly the way she'd planned— about twelve years old. Perfect. Maybe a little bow in her hair. No, that would be overdoing it.

She had both dreaded and longed for this evening to arrive. How could one man incite such opposite emotions? But the peach dress was an inspiration. Drew's friends would wonder what he was doing with such an innocent young thing at this stage in his life. Maybe they'd even accuse him of robbing the cradle. Cassie wanted to see him squirm.

She also wanted to see him, period. She hated to admit how much.

At a quarter to seven, Grammy Jo appeared in her bedroom doorway. "That's what you're wearing?"

"Like it?" Cassie twirled, and the gathered cotton skirt billowed like a sail.

"I would have loved it on you fifteen years ago. Where'd you buy it, in the children's department?"

"As a matter of fact, yes. That's an advantage of being short. If the bodice has lots of pleats, I can still wear a size fourteen."

"What's wrong with the red dress?"

"I found out Drew adores the little-girl look, and his favorite color is peach."

Grammy Jo frowned. "I gave him credit for more taste than that."

"Don't you think I should dress to please him?" Cassie tried to look guileless, which wasn't difficult considering her outfit.

But Grammy Jo wasn't fooled. "Cassie Larue, you're up to something. I can see it in your eyes. Are you playing games with that poor man?"

"Me?"

"You'll be sorry if you mess around and lose him, girl. He could be the best thing you'll ever see."

"I doubt it," Cassie said with as much conviction as she could muster.

"If I were in your shoes, although I wouldn't be caught dead in those cute little flats, I wouldn't be so flip. Men like Drew don't come along every day, and I speak from years of observation, if not experience."

"You really like Drew, don't you?"

"Yes, I do. If someone like Drew, only older, walked into my life, I'd grab him. And I wouldn't play games, as I suspect you're doing."

Cassie thought of A.W. and the moment of destiny that was only minutes away for Grammy Jo. That meeting was the most important aspect of tonight's event. Seeing Drew again was not. She needed to forget about her own miserable love life and focus on her primary goal—bringing A.W. and Grammy Jo together.

She longed to tell Grammy Jo that A.W. had driven over from Phoenix and would be at the party, but she didn't dare. Grammy Jo knew her too well, and the entire plan would be revealed in no time. The older woman might even refuse to go tonight.

"You look terrific, Grammy Jo," she remarked instead. "That material is positively iridescent."

Her grandmother posed with one hand behind her head and the other on her hip. "Don't I look smashing? I would never have had the nerve to buy a clingy jump suit like this when your grandfather was alive. But I wasn't doing aerobics then, and my fanny would have wobbled, anyway."

"It certainly doesn't now." Cassie could hardly wait for A.W. to get an eyeful of her grandmother in the green-and-lavender print that mimicked a snakeskin and shimmered when she walked.

"You're sure you want to wear that dress?" Grammy Jo narrowed her eyes at Cassie. "You look like a vestal virgin." She sniffed suspiciously. "And that perfume smells like some I bought when you were in grade school."

"It is. They still sell it in the preteen cosmetic department."

"Cassie, put on the red dress."

"Nope. And we have to leave, or we'll be late."

"Couldn't you at least unfasten the top few buttons? And put on a tad more makeup? How about some hoop earrings?"

"Nope."

Grammy Jo sighed. "All right. I hope you know what you're doing."

I'm finding a man for you, Cassie thought. *The rest of this nonsense is my way of preserving my sanity. What's left of it.* "I know what I'm doing," she said. "Let's go."

Cassie felt strange, wheeling up to Drew's house in

her Toyota instead of the postal Jeep. Several cars were parked around the circular drive, including A.W.'s green MG.

"Cute car," Grammy Jo commented as they walked past the tiny convertible. "Did I tell you I've been thinking of trading in my Oldsmobile for a sports car?"

"Doesn't surprise me," Cassie said with a smile. This meeting between her grandmother and A.W. was so right she almost hugged herself with satisfaction.

Drew answered the door, a host's jovial smile plastered on his face. His smile brightened when he saw Grammy Jo, but his expression changed to complete bewilderment when Cassie stepped forward.

She would have laughed if her heart hadn't been beating so fast at seeing Drew again. He wore a white linen sport coat over a deep blue shirt and tan slacks. And Grammy Jo was right. Men like Drew didn't come along every day.

He opened his mouth and closed it again. Finally he managed a one-word comment. "Peach."

"I bought it right after our little conversation," Cassie said, batting her eyelashes at him. "When you mentioned how you felt about the color."

Grammy Jo took his arm and pulled him aside. "Convince her to burn that dress," she said in an undertone. "You seem to have an influence over what she wears."

"Not me." Drew shook his head as he stared at a sweetly smiling Cassie, a Cassie who could walk into a high-school classroom with a load of books in her arms and never be questioned. Where was his strawberry-blond bombshell, his tiny package of TNT? "I, uh, guess we might as well go in and meet everyone," he said slowly.

"Peachy!" Cassie said with a flash of dimples and a toss of her head.

Drew groaned. "Good God."

With raised eyebrows Grammy Jo looked from Drew to Cassie. As she followed her granddaughter into the house, she said in a soft little singsong, "I think you're crazy."

Cassie didn't answer. She was searching the crowded living room for A.W. She found him deep in conversation with two women. Of course. *They'd better be married to two of the men here*, she thought murderously, *because if Drew invited any competition for Grammy Jo...*

"Yes, they're married," Drew said into her ear as he saw the direction of her gaze. "I don't go around sabotaging situations, unlike some people I might mention. Incidentally, you smell like the first girl I ever kissed." Without missing a beat he took Grammy Jo's elbow and placed his hand at Cassie's waist. "Come on, you two," he said in a louder voice. "Let's circulate."

Cassie had to admire the way Drew orchestrated the eventual meeting between A.W. and Grammy Jo. He guided his two charges from group to group, deliberately leaving A.W. until the last of the introductions so that once they reached him, Grammy Jo wouldn't have any reason to leave his company.

As Drew presented his friends, Cassie realized from their comments that several of them were ex-convicts attending the party with their wives or girlfriends. They viewed Cassie's demure outfit with curiosity, and she felt certain Drew would be in for some ribbing later. The prospect was comforting.

Gradually Cassie became aware that Drew was directing their progress around the room so that A.W. had plenty of opportunities to notice Grammy Jo. In Cassie's opinion, he noticed. In fact, he seemed to have lost all interest in the conversation of his two companions as he waited for Drew to bring the attractive woman in the jump suit around to his corner of the room.

Just before they arrived, A.W. straightened his tie and smoothed his hair. Then he casually excused himself from his two female companions and sauntered over. No doubt he wanted to be all alone when he met the lady in the jump suit. Cassie had to bite her tongue to keep from laughing in triumph. Now if only Grammy Jo would be equally fascinated!

Drew was magnificently casual. "Oh, there you are, Gramps. I wondered where you were hiding."

A.W. came over to hug Cassie. "Had to say hello to my favorite girl," he said. "I decided you were never going to rescue me from those two biddies," he added in a low voice.

Cassie grinned. "A.W., I'd like you to meet Jo Reynolds, my grandmother. A.W.'s here for the Balloon Fiesta, Grammy Jo."

The older woman flicked the merest glance at Cassie before extending her hand to A.W. "The man with the crickets. And may I congratulate you on a clever ploy."

A.W. looked startled.

"Come on, A.W.," Grammy Jo teased. "I don't believe the exterminator story for a minute. Either you had a hot date that night, or you were smart enough to realize these two young people needed to be alone."

The older man recovered quickly and winked at Grammy Jo. "And a gentleman wouldn't admit which reason it was."

"Doesn't matter," Grammy Jo said with a chuckle. "You were a marvelous cupid, whether you intended to be or not. Congratulations. I've been trying to get this granddaughter of mine hooked up with a man for ages."

Cassie clenched her jaw in frustration but couldn't think of an appropriate comment to silence her grandmother.

Drew put an arm around Cassie's waist. "Thank God you didn't succeed in finding anyone for her until I came along," he said, drawing her close to his side. "Right, Cassie?"

Cassie's heartbeat thundered in her ears as Drew's body pressing against hers brought back all the riotous emotions of their night together. "Right," she said, not daring to look at him. She feared her expression would reveal far too much about her inner turmoil.

"If you'll excuse us for a moment," Drew continued, "I have something to discuss with Cassie. Gramps, would you mind fixing Jo a drink?"

"My pleasure." A.W. cupped Grammy Jo's elbow. "If you like martinis, Jo, I mix them very dry."

Grammy Jo arched one eyebrow. "I bet you do. Something tells me I'd better supervise the process."

Cassie glanced from one to the other in delight. They were flirting with each other! But she barely had time to enjoy her feeling of success before Drew propelled her down the hall and into a room that looked like his office.

"Drew, what about your guests?" she protested as he closed the door behind them.

"They won't make off with the silverware, if that's what you mean."

"I'm sure they won't."

"Most of them went to jail for killing someone, not stealing."

"Don't be ridiculous, Drew. I only meant that you're the host of the party and you have certain duties."

"Damn the duties." He strode forward and took her in his arms. "Damn this whole crazy charade we've been playing."

If he'd been more tentative, Cassie might have been able to stop the kiss, but nothing in his manner asked permission. He took, and she had no time to rally her defenses, to keep herself from giving him all that he demanded and more.

His mustache feathered her lips as his mouth found hers with familiar certainty. Deftly his tongue probed with the determination of a man who has known the secrets of a woman's body and wants to remind her of the pleasures he's shared, the privileges he's enjoyed.

But Cassie needed no reminder. During all the days that they'd been apart, she'd been able to deny the strength of her desire. But now her passion for him gained momentum from that deprivation, and nothing mattered but the exquisite pleasure of his touch.

With a moan she pressed against him, bringing herself into contact with the pulsing warmth of his groin. He reached down and pulled her in even tighter, imprinting his need as he ravaged her mouth.

She forgot the houseful of people. She forgot her grandmother and A.W. She was a woman propelled by overwhelming needs that surged through her and settled like molten lava in the throbbing center of her being.

When he lifted his head, he was breathing hard. "The dress didn't work."

She struggled to make sense of his words. "What do you mean?" she murmured through swollen lips.

"If you thought the Shirley Temple act would turn me off, it didn't work." His chest heaved. "And the little-girl perfume. That really backfired."

"I..." She tried to remember just what she'd meant to accomplish with the peach dress and the faint flowery scent. He nipped her earlobe and boldly stroked her breast through the cotton material of the dress. "You smell just like Mary Jane."

"Who?"

"My girlfriend in sixth grade. But I didn't have the nerve to touch Mary Jane the way I'm touching you."

She gazed wordlessly up at him as his supple fingers worked their magic and she became warm and pliant in his arms.

"Cassie, my little schoolgirl," he murmured, watching her reaction to his caress. "There's something very provocative about the innocent look when I know you're not." His dark eyes were hot with desire as he undid the buttons at her neck. "Hell, you even look good in peach. I didn't think anyone did."

A part of her brain remembered the party in progress outside his study door. "Drew, maybe you shouldn't..."

"Probably not." He kept unbuttoning. "Want to stop me, Cassie?"

She opened her mouth, but no sound came out.

"I didn't think so." He unfastened the front clasp of her bra and pushed the material away to expose her gleaming breasts, their tips rigid with arousal. With a sigh he bent to take one aching nipple in his mouth, and Cassie arched her back and gave herself up to the glorious sensation of being loved by Drew, of experiencing the sensual brush of his beard against her heated skin.

He sucked each breast tenderly, and she could feel his body quivering with passion as he caressed her. "You taste like peaches," he murmured against her skin. "God, I want to love you all over. I've missed you. Missed this."

"Drew." She gasped as her knees threatened to give way, and she clutched his shoulders for support. "You're driving me crazy."

"I'm glad." He lifted his head and pressed kisses on her closed eyelids. "And I'm driving myself crazy. But this isn't the time or place." With trembling fingers he pulled the material of her bra to cover the pale globes still damp from his kisses. "I...I can't make love to you now," he said raggedly, fumbling with the bra's clasp. "Stay after the party's over, Cassie. Stay with me tonight."

Cassie's heart pounded out a demanding rhythm as he rebuttoned the front of the peach dress. He was right. Making love now, during the party, would have been crazy. But what about the horrible ache inside her? "Drew..." she moaned.

"I know," he said gently. "I'm in bad shape, too. I

shouldn't have started something we couldn't finish, but I've been out of my head with wanting to kiss you, touch you, again. At least I know you still feel the same way."

Slowly reason returned. She hadn't meant for anything like this to happen. "I probably shouldn't feel that way. I...wish I didn't."

"Don't wish that, Cassie. We can work things out, I promise. Just don't shut me out. Stay tonight. Let me love you again."

She clung to his statement that they could work things out. Had he reconsidered his stand? "Drew, I came to the party with Grammy Jo. I can't let her go home alone. Besides, your grandfather will be here tonight."

Drew smiled. "Maybe not. You saw the way those two reacted to each other. What if we suggest to Gramps that he take your grandmother home?"

"But they just met!"

"Cassie Larue, are you going to impose a code of conduct on our grandparents?"

"Of course not, but I don't think they should spend the night together before they've gotten to know each other."

"Spending the night together is a great way to become acquainted. I'll vouch for that, won't you?"

"We had a date first," Cassie said. She also remembered that she'd given her passion full rein before she'd understood Drew's feelings about handwriting analysis. And now she had a mess on her hands.

"Yes, we had a date, but we're younger and have more time for the preliminaries. Besides, Gramps and Jo may not end up in bed together just because he takes her home. They may go out for coffee or sit and talk all night.''

"Sure. Your grandfather is a known womanizer."

"I beg your pardon?"

"You said yourself he's had lots of women on the string since your grandmother died."

"So he has, but Jo's an adult. She can handle herself. Cassie, our goal was to bring these two people together, and now you're not willing to let nature take its course."

"Nature can take its course. It's A.W.'s course I'm worried about."

"All right. Suppose I suggest he take her out for coffee. I'll quietly let him know that you'll be home in a couple of hours. Your threatened presence should keep him honest, but we'll have a little privacy ourselves over here."

The thought of being alone with Drew was so tempting that Cassie shivered. "I never thought of myself as a chaperone for my grandmother," she said to cover her reaction.

"Well, consider that you might be. And if you don't get out of the way for a little while, Gramps and Jo may not have an opportunity to fall madly in love."

Madly in love. Yes, I am, Drew. Lord help me. "You're very persuasive, Dr. Bennett."

He studied her expression for any evidence that she was using his title sarcastically. But her attitude was open and trusting, as it had been before they'd argued about her handwriting analysis.

Drew didn't have the answer to that disagreement yet. He had tried to read the first book in his stack from the library, but the subject still seemed like mystical hocus-pocus to him. Perhaps if he and Cassie could enjoy a night of serious loving, the handwriting problem would fade in significance for both of them. He prayed that A.W. would indeed squire Grammy Jo home.

With a smile he adjusted the prim collar of her dress and rubbed his thumb across her kiss-reddened lips. She looked a little mussed, but the people outside the door would expect that.

As the edge of his passion dulled, he again became aware of the muffled sounds of the party progressing in the next room. He and Cassie had been gone long enough. After all, he was the host, as she had said.

"I guess we'd better mingle," he said, touching her cheek tenderly. "Tell me you'll stay for a while after the party, and I'll return to my duties...somehow."

"It depends on Grammy Jo."

"If she agrees to go out for coffee with Gramps, you'll stay?"

Cassie was gazing up at him, assent shining in her hazel eyes, when the sound of two angry voices could be heard above the general hum of party conversation. "That sounds like Grammy Jo," she whispered.

"And Gramps. Damn." He started for the door as the argument rose in volume. The two people who were supposed to stick together like glue tonight and leave him alone with Cassie were fighting like banshees. What had gone wrong? When he and Cassie left, they had seemed tickled pink with each other. "They're in the kitchen," he said over his shoulder and led the way.

As he walked through the entrance to the kitchen, he could tell the situation was bad.

Jo stood facing A.W., hands on her hips and chin

lifted. Her blue eyes flashed at him. "And furthermore, size is unimportant to me!" she said vehemently.

"You women always say that, but you're not telling the truth," A.W. shot back. "When you get down to the nitty-gritty, size matters a hell of a lot to you."

"Oh, so we're liars, are we?"

"On that subject you are."

Drew paused in amazed discomfort. Certainly they weren't arguing about... No, not these two grandparents! But he didn't have the courage to ask. "Uh, can I freshen anyone's drink?"

Cassie appeared beside him. He glanced down and noticed her cheeks were rosy. Had she heard this strange interchange between A.W. and Grammy Jo? Did she think they were referring to what he thought they were referring to?

"I don't care for anything else to drink," the older woman said haughtily. "And I especially don't want to drink with this fellow."

Cassie looked at the couple in dismay. "A.W., there are some delicious-looking sandwiches in the other room. Why don't we go get a plateful, and the four of us can—"

A.W. straightened his shoulders and turned to her with a dignified little bow. "Thank you, Cassie, but the lady and I have agreed to disagree. We won't be sharing sandwiches—or anything else this evening."

"That's terrible!" Cassie tried to think of a way to smooth over the argument, but she was embarrassed to begin. From what she'd heard, they were arguing about something very personal. "I'm sure after you both have a chance to cool down, you'll reconsider," she said lamely.

"I doubt it, Cassie," Grammy Jo said. "In fact, I'd like to go home. I'm sure Drew will bring you later if you care to stay. Just loan me the keys to your car, and I'll be on my way."

Drew stepped forward. "I really wish you wouldn't leave, Jo. This, uh, misunderstanding between you and Gramps can be cleared up. Let's all have another drink and something to eat. Then we'll—"

"You're a sweetheart, Drew." Grammy Jo patted his bearded cheek. "But I'm leaving." She threw a defiant glance at A.W. "Before he can make any more insulting remarks."

"Then I'm leaving, too," Cassie said. "I think my purse is in the hall, Grammy Jo."

"You really don't have to go with me, Cassie."

"No, it's...it's probably best." She ignored the pleading look on Drew's face. "Go ahead and start the car. I'll be right out."

"Cassie." Drew caught her arm and brought her close to his side. "Stay, anyway. I don't care about proprieties. This is important."

"Grammy Jo's upset. That's important, too," Cassie said, reluctantly pulling away from him. "I can't let her go home alone."

"Then come back later. I'll be awake."

"No, Drew." With one last backward glance she hurried out of the kitchen.

When she got in the car, Grammy Jo gunned the engine and churned out of the driveway, sending gravel in all directions. Cassie gripped the armrest and thought of the way A.W. drove his MG compared to the way Grammy Jo was driving tonight. Their style was very similar.

"That arrogant man," Grammy Jo mumbled to herself. "Thinks he knows everything. Well, he's dead wrong about this."

Cassie cleared her throat. Curiosity got the best of her, and she decided to find out for sure if Grammy Jo and A.W. had been arguing about what she suspected they'd been arguing about. "What were you two, uh, discussing?"

"Discussing? That was a full-scale fight, in case you didn't notice."

"I noticed."

"That man has some nerve!"

"Does he?" Cassie wondered how to ask her question again. She and her grandmother were close, but they'd never talked about their preference in men's...

"He certainly does." Grammy Jo screeched to a stop at a red light. "Tell me, Cassie. Do you care about size?"

Cassie's face grew hot. Where was this role as cupid leading her? "I, uh, don't know that I—"

"See? I told that jackass that women don't care if Robert Redford is short."

7

CASSIE STARED at her grandmother across the dark interior of the car. "You were fighting about Robert Redford's height?"

"We were talking about movies. I merely asked him what he thought of Robert Redford's acting ability."

Cassie groaned. There was only one right answer to that question as far as Grammy Jo was concerned.

"He said Robert Redford's acting was okay. *Okay*. And then he made some remark about Redford's size. By that time I was livid."

"I can imagine." Cassie shook her head. It was almost funny. If she weren't so damn frustrated about the way the evening was turning out for her and Grammy Jo, she would laugh. Instead, she ground her back teeth. She'd always liked Redford, but tonight he wasn't her favorite Hollywood star.

"I think Drew's grandfather is extremely insecure. He can't admit Robert Redford is a gorgeous hunk for fear he'll look bad in comparison. It's so stupid—a man with A.W.'s distinguished good looks, intimidated by a man probably neither of us will ever meet."

Cassie sat straighter in the seat. "Did you tell him he was good-looking?"

"Certainly not. Not after he didn't have the decency to acknowledge another man's talent. You should have seen A.W. when I mentioned how much I admired

Redford. He squared those broad shoulders of his, puffed out his chest and said, 'He isn't very tall, is he?' I could have punched him."

"Broad shoulders?" Cassie smiled. Maybe all wasn't lost.

"I wouldn't expect you to notice A.W.'s broad shoulders with your absorption in Drew. I suppose that's why you didn't mention what a good-looking grandfather Drew had when you got back from Phoenix. I've been curious about him ever since you told me about the cricket hoax."

"You still don't believe that?"

"Cassie, he could have postponed the exterminator's visit to another day when he found out you were coming."

"But he'd made plans to stay overnight with some old friends. He couldn't cancel that."

"They would have understood, unless, of course, *they* was a *she*. A.W. is a very virile man, Cassie."

"Do you think so?"

"Extremely virile." Grammy Jo's driving slowed to a more normal pace. "And sexy," she said again, softly. Then she smacked the steering wheel. "With a damn fragile ego! Thank God he lives in Phoenix, and I won't have to see him again."

"Right." Cassie was glad the darkness hid her gleeful expression from Grammy Jo.

The two women spent the rest of the drive talking about Drew's strange assortment of guests. They compared notes and decided that, in addition to exconvicts, Drew had invited several law-enforcement types.

"It was a strange brew, all right," Grammy Jo concluded as they unlocked the front door and walked into the house. "I'm sorry I dragged you away early. That was selfish of me, but I didn't know any other way to make my point than to leave."

Cassie nodded, familiar with her grandmother's love of dramatic gestures. "I have to get up early for work, anyway, Grammy Jo," she said, trying to mute her own disappointment and convince herself that leaving Drew tonight had been the wise thing to do.

"How long is that man staying? Not that I really care."

"Who?" Cassie pretended that all thought of A.W. had vanished from her mind.

"That irritating grandfather of Drew's."

Cassie coughed to hide the laughter that she couldn't suppress anymore. "At least through the weekend. He wants to see the Balloon Fiesta, as I mentioned before. Maybe even take a ride in a hot-air balloon."

"Does he?" Grammy Jo's face brightened until she remembered to scowl. "Damn," she muttered as she trailed into her bedroom. "I thought you and I might go out there ourselves, and now I have to worry about running into that infuriating fellow."

I'll make sure you do, Cassie decided. Unless, of course, A.W. was turned off by Grammy Jo's staunch defense of her hero, Robert Redford. Grammy Jo was still very intrigued by Drew's grandfather. Cassie hoped the interest remained mutual.

The only way to find out was to contact Drew. Cassie decided to call him on her lunch hour the following day. She pretended the call was for her grandmother's sake, but honesty finally prompted her to admit that she would have searched for some excuse to call him, anyway.

The attraction between them was too powerful to dismiss easily; she had realized that after their passionate encounter in his office during the party. Although their difference of opinion hadn't been settled, Cassie interpreted Drew's behavior to mean that he was on the verge of apologizing for his remarks in Phoenix.

She imagined a scene in which he acknowledged the professionalism of graphoanalysis and listened with approval as she explained her methods. If he understood the analysis process and viewed her painstaking calculations, his attitude would certainly be different. A man who kissed like Drew couldn't be completely pigheaded, could he?

Her call reached Drew's answering machine. Why had she assumed he would be home, waiting for her to phone? She hung up in frustration but then remembered that the answering machine might be the only way she could contact him if he was out showing A.W. the sights of Albuquerque. She dialed again and left a brief message for him to call her that evening.

THE TELEPHONE WAS RINGING when she walked in the door after work, and she heard Grammy Jo answer it.

"Why, hello, Drew! How's my second favorite sex symbol?" Grammy Jo chuckled at Drew's response. "I think she just arrived. Listen, your party was lovely, and I apologize for leaving so early. But I'm sure you all had a great time, anyway." She paused again. "Oh, he didn't? What a shame." Grammy Jo winked at Cassie. "Nope, haven't given that silly fight a moment's thought. Well, here's your sweetheart."

Cassie took the receiver eagerly. "Hello?"

"Have dinner with me," he said, his voice low and desperate. "I'm going out of my mind. I wanted to call you today, but you were at work, and Gramps insisted on taking the Tramway up the mountain and eating lunch in Old Town—and God knows what else he would have us doing if I hadn't put my foot down."

"Can you leave him to have dinner with me?"

"You bet your booties I can. I told him to order out for pizza, and I've rented three sex comedies for the VCR."

"That sounds like the kind of plans you'd make for a teenager."

"I swear that's what he's like! I've got to talk to you alone, but more than that, I've got to see you. Whoops, he just walked into the room. I'll pick you up at eight."

Cassie slowly hung up the phone, savoring the thought of dinner with the man she loved. Dinner and...

"Cassie, your dimples are showing."

"Are they?"

"You're going to see Drew tonight, aren't you?"

"Yes."

"Tell him for me that his grandfather's an old coot."

"I will not, Grammy Jo."

"So what's A.W. doing with himself tonight, if you're going out with Drew?"

Cassie eyed her grandmother. "Pizza and rented movies on the VCR." She decided against mentioning the sex comedies.

"Alone?"

"As far as I know. Care to drive over and join him?"

"Absolutely not! I was curious, that's all. He's probably picked out movies where the women all have big bazooms and the men can't act their way out of a paper bag."

Cassie pressed her lips together to keep from laughing. Grammy Jo had the man pegged. "You don't think he'll watch Robert Redford tonight, Grammy Jo?" she teased.

Her grandmother snorted. "No, but I will. Now go on and take your bubble bath or whatever ritual you always go through for a date. And don't come home early, either. And don't wear that god-awful peach dress!"

Cassie hadn't planned to wear the peach dress. Or the little-girl scent. She piled her hair on top of her head, attached glittering earrings to her earlobes and sprayed a sinfully decadent fragrance all over her nude body. Then she donned lace panties, her red dress and red high-heeled sandals. No bra, no panty hose, no slip. She felt sexy as the devil as her smooth-shaven legs whispered against the silken lining of the eyelet skirt.

"NOW THAT'S MORE LIKE IT," Drew murmured as he helped her into the Audi, and his hand cupped her elbow a little longer than necessary.

Cassie smiled, enjoying the desire shining in Drew's eyes. What a glorious thing, this passion that flared between them. Cassie felt sorry for anyone who had never experienced the mindless abandon that swept over her whenever Drew touched her.

"We need to talk about A.W. and Grammy Jo," she said reluctantly when he got into the car and started the engine. She didn't want to talk about their grandparents. She didn't want to talk at all.

His glance told her that he also longed to do something besides talk. "I guess."

"Did you find out what they were fighting about?"

"Yep. I was sure they were shouting about a very delicate subject."

"So was I."

Drew chuckled. "I'm supposed to be the psychologist, unflappable in any circumstances, impossible to shock. But when I walked in and heard Grammy Jo bellowing that size didn't matter to women and Gramps insisting that it did, I hadn't the faintest idea how to make a graceful transition to another topic."

"I loved your first line—'Can I freshen anyone's drink?'" Cassie shook with laughter. "I wish I'd had a tape recorder."

"You weren't much better, suggesting a nice plate of sandwiches. I'm beginning to think we're bigger prudes than they are."

"Maybe, but it's still our job to get them back together."

"You think we can?"

"Yes. Grammy Jo complained about A.W. all the way home last night, but I think she's dying to see him again. When we compared A.W. to a teenager, I realized that's how she's behaving, too. The more she talks about how terrible your grandfather is, the more I'm convinced she's hooked on him."

"Gramps has been doing the same thing, referring every five minutes to his disdain for that 'hauty Reynolds woman,' and then he'll ask if I noticed what a great figure she has. Drives me nuts."

"We've got to arrange another meeting, Drew."

He sighed. "I was afraid this wouldn't be as easy as it sounded at first. Any ideas?"

"Grammy Jo gave me the perfect excuse for a chance encounter. How about each of us taking them to the sunrise ascension of the balloons on Saturday? You know what she did? She pretended to be worried that she'd run into A.W. at the balloon festival. What a broad hint!"

"Okay, we'll do it."

"Do you think A.W. will have sense enough to stay away from the topic of Robert Redford?"

"Good Lord, I hope so. Is there anything else your grandmother gets on her high horse about?"

"She's become quite a feminist. But I've never heard A.W. complain about women's liberation."

"He wouldn't. Grammy Jo's modern outlook is one of the things that I figured would bring them together. He doesn't expect his wife to be his maid. That's one reason he's so popular with women."

"Okay. We should be fine. And Drew?"

"Yes?"

"This will be it, I promise. If the dose doesn't take the second time, we'll give up."

"That's a deal. I only hope I can live through the next two days with Gramps. He wants to see your grandmother again in the worst way, but his pride won't allow him to call. He's no fun these days, and all he wants to do is tear around Albuquerque in that little car of his. And take me with him so he can talk to someone about Jo."

"Are you sure he's a careful driver?"

Drew glanced at her. "Worried about me?"

"Could be."

"That's good. By the way, I'm not taking the sleeping pills that you recommended, Cassie."

"I wish you would. If you're not sleeping well, that is."

"I certainly didn't last night."

"Thinking about A.W. and Grammy Jo?"

They stopped at a red light, and he gave her a long look. "No, I wasn't. I have other things on my mind." He swung the Audi into the parking lot of one of Albuquerque's major hotels.

Cassie turned to him and raised her eyebrows.

"I hear the food's good in the restaurant," he said with a shrug as he parked the car. After they were seated, he excused himself for a moment.

Cassie said nothing, but she didn't miss how Drew's gaze lingered on the bodice of the dress when he returned.

Later, as they sipped cocktails and waited for their dinner, Drew brought up the subject of the party.

"You'll be glad to know I caught it from all sides after you left," he said, leaning toward her. "I couldn't convince a single person there except Gramps, who'd seen you dressed normally, that you're twenty-five. They don't think you're past the age of consent."

Cassie grinned. "I suppose it was a dirty trick."

"When I saw you standing in the doorway in that peach dress, I knew you must be furious with me."

"I was."

"And now?"

Cassie knew she should bring up the subject of handwriting analysis and find out if Drew had changed his mind. But how she hated to disturb the warm current of emotion flowing between them. "What do you think?"

"You didn't wear the peach dress tonight."

"No."

They were silent for several minutes as they gazed into each other's eyes. Then he reached into his pocket. "The truth is, I don't know a thing about the food here," he said, placing a room key on the table between them.

THE SKY WAS PUSSY-WILLOW GRAY when Drew walked Cassie to the door of her grandmother's house and turned the key in the lock.

"I feel guilty," he murmured, putting the key back in her hand. "You have to work today, and all I have to do is tolerate Gramps."

"It's not quite five," Cassie whispered back. "I can sleep for a couple of hours."

He pulled her close and tipped her face up to gaze into her eyes. "I wish I could sleep beside you."

"So do I."

"I bet Jo wouldn't mind." He brushed her lips gently with his.

"Probably not, but I would."

"I do believe you're more old-fashioned than your grandmother," he teased.

She reached out to stroke his beard. "Maybe."

"I think I like that." He kissed the pads of her fingers. "I won't see you until tomorrow morning? That's a long time."

"I know." Cassie sighed and nestled against him.

"My racquetball game is going to hell."

She chuckled. "We wouldn't stop with racquetball,

and you know it. We both need our sleep so we'll be sharp for tomorrow. A lot rests on this so-called chance meeting."

His body tensed slightly. "How much, Cassie?"

"Why, their future, of course."

"And ours?"

Cassie laid her ear against his chest and listened to the steady beat of his heart. So much hadn't been discussed tonight; instead, their bodies had clamored for a release that could not be denied any longer. Drew and Cassie had been too busy loving each other to talk about anything.

Her graphoanalysis was still an unresolved issue, but Drew had raised another one. What if A.W. and Grammy Jo decided not to become a couple? Would she leave Grammy Jo to a lonely existence in order to be with Drew?

She lifted her head and looked into eyes filled with frustration and uncertainty. "No," she said softly. "Our future has nothing to do with theirs anymore."

"Thank God." He kissed her hungrily, even though they'd just spent hours exploring the depths of their passion. And still he wanted her. Once this business with their grandparents was settled, one way or another he'd work to put his relationship with Cassie on firmer ground. Right now, with a chaperone in each house, a love affair wasn't easy to engineer.

Reluctantly he released her, noting with masculine pride that her cheeks were flushed and her breathing as labored as his. "You'd better go in. You'd think after tonight I'd be completely satiated, but..." He shrugged helplessly.

"I'm glad you're not," she said softly, forcing herself

to draw away from his warmth. For the first time she noticed the chill of the early morning and shivered.

"It's cold. Go on in," he urged, not moving from his spot.

"I don't want to leave you."

He groaned and reached for her. "Oh, Cassie." His swift and forceful kiss left them both trembling with renewed desire. "Now...go," he said unsteadily.

They exchanged another long look before she opened the door and closed it behind her without a word.

Drew walked slowly back to his car. Once inside, he sat with his arms draped over the steering wheel and waited for his body to calm down. God, she was something! At last he put the car in gear and drove away, heading for his house on the bluffs west of town.

He'd never forget how Cassie's eyes had glowed with anticipation when he'd placed the hotel-room key on the white linen cloth.

The meal had become a necessary chore then, and they'd left half the dinner on their plates. After paying the check Drew had circled Cassie's waist with his arm and forced them both to saunter through the restaurant and into a waiting elevator.

As Drew remembered what had happened after that, he sat through an entire green-light cycle at an intersection. Only when the light flashed red once more did he start guiltily and look around. Fortunately, there were no cars behind him at this early hour. He shook his head ruefully. And he'd criticized his grandfather's driving.

He concentrated on the red light, but the color brought Cassie right back. That red dress. All through dinner he'd watched the shadowed hint of bare skin beneath the lacings of her dress. When at last he'd been able to untie the bow and pull the lacings free...

A horn bleated behind the Audi, and Drew stepped on the gas. Good thing he wasn't flying today. He was menace enough on the road.

Finally he pulled into his driveway. In only a matter of hours, Cassie would come along in her little Jeep with a handful of his mail. Drew considered being there when she drove up. Wouldn't a fleeting glimpse of those dimples be better than nothing until Saturday morning?

Then he remembered he'd promised A.W. they'd go up to Santa Fe today. If he begged off, his grandfather would be in a more difficult mood than he was already. If Grammy Jo didn't take A.W. off his hands on Saturday, he might have to invent an excuse to leave town himself.

And take Cassie with him. Cassie of the full, pouting breasts with nipples like wild strawberries. Now that he'd known the wonders of her compact little body, he couldn't imagine why taller women used to appeal to him so much. Everything about Cassie was so neatly accessible.

Except she wasn't particularly accessible now, miles away in her grandmother's house. He had to get Cassie separated from her grandmother. If A.W. wasn't the answer, then he'd just have to... Have to what?

Go ahead and admit it, Bennett. You're on the brink of a serious move here. But he hadn't even decided if he loved her. Or had he? What else was love if not this all-consuming need to be with her, to hear her voice, feel her touch?

Drew quietly let himself into the house and walked into his bedroom. Still fully clothed, he lay on his back on the king-sized bed that this morning seemed far too large for one person. Was he ready to get married again? He stared at the beamed ceiling and thought about it.

MILES AWAY, Cassie also lay wide awake, unable to forget the night's events long enough to drift into sleep. Finally she gave up and wandered into the kitchen for a glass of orange juice.

On the table was her mail from the day before. She'd been so excited about the date with Drew that she hadn't bothered to pick it up when she'd gotten home. She poured herself a glass of juice and sat down with the letter opener.

Cassie sorted through the envelopes, choosing which one to open first. When she saw Evan's letter, there was no contest. She slit the envelope and pulled out a long, typed message. *Of course he would type it*, she thought with a smile.

Eagerly scanning the letter, Cassie gasped. Evan's client was an accused murderer! Yet she'd seen nothing in his script to indicate he could commit such a violent crime. There wasn't enough force in his handwriting to suggest that he would hurt anyone. She had formed a picture of a timid, shy man with low goals and little initiative. He was honest and frank, although others might have trouble learning that characteristic because he wasn't very talkative. He couldn't be guilty of murder. Cassie was ninety-nine percent sure of it.

Evan explained more about the case and said he was working with the defense attorney to prove the man's innocence. After receiving her thorough analysis Evan was convinced his client hadn't committed a crime. And he wanted to pay her for her work.

Cassie stared at the letter, wondering what Drew's reaction would be to reading it. And he would read it, she decided.

An hour later, Grammy Jo entered the kitchen and found her still contemplating Evan's letter.

"What have you got there?" Grammy Jo asked, peering over Cassie's shoulders.

"The psychologist at ASU, Drew's friend, is using my analysis of a client's handwriting to help clear him of a murder charge."

"How exciting!"

"On top of that, I'm supposed to submit a bill for my work."

"Then do it. You deserve every penny, I'm sure."

"I only intended to do a favor for Drew's friend."

"Nevertheless, Cassie, you are a professional. So act like one and submit that bill. This psychologist will respect you more if you put a worth on what you do."

"Maybe so. But I'm going to discuss it with Drew. I don't want him to think I used the trip as a chance to drum up business."

"Drew knows about your graphoanalysis, then."

"Yes."

"I assume he's supportive."

Cassie rested her chin in her hands. "He...he's a little skeptical. He needs to learn more about it."

Grammy Jo grinned. "Did you spend some time instructing him last night?"

Cassie looked sheepish. "You heard me come in, I take it."

"I didn't mean to, but after all the years of sleeping in this house, I hear every strange noise. Your mother didn't appreciate that fact while she was still at home dating your father."

"I hope I didn't disturb you."

Grammy Jo patted her hand. "Not a bit. I'm delighted with this romance. Drew's good for you. Too bad he has such an obnoxious grandfather, though."

The reference to A.W. reminded Cassie of the plan she and Drew had cooked up. But she had to wait until later to suggest it, or Grammy Jo would figure out the connection between going to watch the balloons and Drew's grandfather.

Casually, as she was leaving for work, she brought up the subject of the Balloon Fiesta. "I'd like to see them take off at sunrise, wouldn't you?" she asked Grammy Jo.

"It would be spectacular, at that."

"How about tomorrow morning?"

"I guess." Grammy Jo poured herself another cup of coffee and winked. "But if you're going out with Drew again tonight, I don't know when you'll sleep."

"We're not going out. Both of us need some sleep, and besides, we'll see each other tomor—uh, soon."

Grammy Jo gave Cassie a piercing look. "Hmm." Then she smiled a secret sort of smile. "In that case, I'd love to watch the balloons lift off tomorrow morning."

Cassie decided her grandmother suspected what was going on. Apparently she didn't mind. Saturday would be a big day, with A.W. and Grammy Jo having another chance and Cassie once again broaching the subject of graphoanalysis to Drew.

She had told her grandmother that he needed to

learn more about handwriting analysis. Maybe now was the time to teach him. She had a photocopy of the writing sample Evan had sent, and she could show it to Drew along with the letter.

After last night Cassie couldn't believe he would have the same attitude as before. Tomorrow seemed as full of gay promise as a sky dotted with multicolored balloons.

8

AT THE CUTTER BALLOONPORT the next morning the whoosh of propane burners and an international mix of languages carried on the sharp, clear air. Shivery with excitement, Cassie and Grammy Jo wandered through the shadowed forest of balloons in various stages of inflation.

Despite the large, cosmopolitan crowd, Cassie had no doubt she and Drew would find each other. She imagined them as somewhat like a male and a female moth, emitting a special scent that would draw them together. She felt radiant with energy, as buoyed up as the rainbow-colored nylon airships rising all around her like giant spinning tops.

"What a fantastic sight, Cassie," Grammy Jo said, gazing up at the polka-dotted sky. "I'd love to ride in one, wouldn't you?"

"Yes. Yes, I would." Cassie gave the soaring balloons a cursory glance and returned her attention to the crowd. When she saw him, bending forward to examine the wicker gondola of a royal-purple balloon, she took an involuntary step forward, as if he held a string to which she was attached.

"Why, there's Drew," she said, trying her best to sound pleasantly surprised.

Grammy Jo lowered her gaze and looked at Cassie.

"What an amazing coincidence," she said with a perfectly straight face.

"A.W.'s with him," Cassie added.

Grammy Jo nodded. "Why do you suppose I wore my best sweater from Sanger-Harris?"

"You knew."

"I not only knew, I planned. You take hints well, sweetheart. Thanks."

"You're welcome."

"Do you think A.W. realizes that you and Drew have been matchmaking?"

"I don't know, Grammy Jo, but the Balloon Fiesta is the last effort on our part, honest. We won't interfere after today."

"You won't have to. I can handle it from here." Grammy Jo took a compact from her purse, checked her lipstick and headed for the purple balloon.

Cassie almost had to run to keep up with her grandmother's long strides, and Grammy Jo reached their destination first.

"Hello, Drew, A.W.," she said with a curt nod. "What an interesting surprise."

A.W. glanced up. He quickly replaced his initial startled look with one of urbane goodwill. "So you enjoy the ballooning experience, as well, Jo?"

"Don't give me that, A.W. I'll bet you've never been up in one of these contraptions."

Cassie looked at Drew and rolled her eyes. Would these two be able to handle a civil conversation?

"I've been waiting for the perfect opportunity," A.W. said smoothly.

"There's no such think as perfection in this world," Grammy Jo countered. "I think you haven't ridden in a balloon because you're a procrastinator or you're scared."

Cassie gasped, but A.W.'s eyes began to sparkle in response to Grammy Jo's goading.

"How about you, Jo? Are you afraid to take a balloon ride?" A.W. asked.

"I'm more afraid of not taking one and missing out on a wonderful thrill."

As Cassie listened to them wrangle, she wondered if they were discussing balloon rides at all. Was Grammy Jo trying to find out if A.W. was willing to take risks?

"Well, Jo, you've got the right attitude," A.W. said. "What is it the kids say? 'No guts, no glory'?"

Grammy Jo stood straighter. "Kids, my eye. *I* still say that. So how about it, A.W.? Think we can find a balloon that will take a couple of passengers?"

"Right here," A.W. replied, sweeping an arm toward the purple balloon. "Drew, would you mind if Jo went up instead of you?"

Cassie suddenly realized Grammy Jo and A.W. were serious about this.

"Sure, Gramps, that's fine," Drew said.

Cassie looked at the gondola that suddenly appeared flimsy and dangerous. "Wait a minute, Grammy Jo," she protested, hurrying forward as her grandmother started to climb into the basket. "Maybe you shouldn't—"

Drew caught her arm. "Let them go," he said gently, guiding her to one side. "Gramps arranged this trip for two people in exchange for his helping with the chase vehicle next week. I intended to give my place to Jo, if she agreed. We hoped for this, remember?"

"But there's no protection up there. They don't wear parachutes or anything!"

"Neither did we in the Cessna."

"But that's different."

"Not really." He put his arms around her waist and pulled her back against his chest. "Look at them, Cassie," he whispered into her ear. "Look at their faces."

Cassie had to admit she'd never seen her grandmother happier, and A.W. was beaming like a kid as he stood beside Grammy Jo in the wicker gondola.

"This ride could be it, Cassie," Drew continued. "A shared unforgettable experience that will bind them together."

"I guess so." Cassie tried to quell her panic as the tethered balloon rose above the ground. "They look so trusting and vulnerable."

"That's when people fall in love, when they're trusting and vulnerable. Wave, Cassie."

Dutifully she lifted her arm and waved.

Grammy Jo waved back. "This is magnificent!" she shouted as the crew released the balloon and it soared gracefully upward.

A.W. put an arm around her and echoed her comment. "Magnificent!" he called, but he was looking at Grammy Jo, not at the panorama spread below him.

"Drew, I love Grammy Jo so much. What if something happens to her because of what I've gotten her into?"

"What if you ignored her and nothing ever happened to her? And I mean nothing—no men in her life, no parties, no balloon trips. You're a positive force in her life, Cassie. But she's a grown-up. She can say no whenever she wants to. Right now she's saying yes, and I think it's great."

"I...I can't see them anymore. The balloon's getting so high and so small."

"They'll be back."

"I know, but..."

"Cassie." He turned her to face him. "Don't chicken out now. You decided several months ago to change the status quo for you and your grandmother. Your efforts are bearing fruit, and that's scary. But change is good, Cassie." He took a deep breath. "God, you're beautiful."

"So are you."

"Come on." He wrapped one arm around her shoulders and guided her away from the spot where the purple balloon had taken off. "Let's see if we can find two hot cups of coffee."

For the next hour they strolled the area, watching other balloons ascend while they talked about the future for A.W. and Grammy Jo.

"I can offer to let Gramps stay with me as long as he likes," Drew said. "They'll probably want some courtship time before they decide if this will lead to anything permanent."

"Probably, but won't that be rough on you, having a houseguest all the time?"

"It will be rough on us, my love. Change 'houseguest' to 'chaperone,' and you have the picture. I was hoping we could stop meeting in hotel rooms, but we may have to sacrifice a little longer for their sakes."

Cassie walked beside him in silence as she pondered the questions his statement raised. Obviously Drew expected their relationship, in all its aspects, to continue.

But on what basis? Were they headed for a prolonged affair with no strings attached, or for something more? Cassie didn't know how to ask, especially in this public place with the impending return of Grammy Jo and A.W.

Drew had called her "my love" more than once, yet he'd never said straight out that he loved her. As for Cassie, *love* was the only word that seemed adequate to describe her feelings for Drew. But before she revealed the extent of her commitment, she wanted some assurance that he would support her ambition to pursue a career in graphoanalysis.

Cassie had tucked Evan's letter and the handwriting sample into her purse that morning. She wasn't sure how the day would turn out or if she'd have a chance to spend several hours alone with Drew, but if the opportunity arose, she planned to discuss the letter with him.

His reaction to her discussion would tell her if her hunch was right and he was willing to change his former antagonistic attitude toward the study of handwriting. Cassie wanted to believe so much that he was.

Drew peered down at her. "You're not talking. Do hotel rooms bother you so much? If so, I'll send Gramps packing and let him conduct his courtship as best he can."

"No, I was just thinking."

"About?"

"Us."

"As well you should. It's time to do an in-depth study of the subject, but I figured we'd wait to see how this morning turned out between Gramps and Grammy Jo. Fair enough?"

She smiled at him. It seemed she couldn't help smiling when he looked at her with those warm brown eyes. "Fair enough."

"And speaking of our favorite senior citizens, here they come, climbing out of that chase car."

"That's right. I forgot they wouldn't come back and land here, like an airplane. Somebody had to bring them back from wherever they touched down."

"Cassie, they're holding hands."

"So they are."

"By George, I think we did it. I'd better plan on a semipermanent houseguest."

"I feel like it's Christmas or something, Drew."

He gave her a quick hug. "Congratulations, Santa Claus."

When Grammy Jo and A.W. approached to within hearing distance, Cassie called out to the blissful couple. "How was it?" she asked unnecessarily. She could see how it was, but she wanted to hear them say it.

"Unbelievable," A.W. called back. "You two have to try it someday."

"We were lucky the pilot agreed to take us up," Grammy Jo said. "A chartered ride costs a lot of money."

"Oh, but it would be worth every penny," A.W. added, glancing at Jo. "Wouldn't you say?"

Grammy Jo gave him a private smile. "Yes."

Cassie wanted to hop up and down with joy. "Did they break out the champagne? I thought they gave you champagne on your first flight."

Grammy Jo chuckled. "No, thank God, because not only do you drink it, but they pour it over you. I would have ruined this good cashmere."

"If you didn't have champagne in the balloon, how about a champagne brunch somewhere?" Drew suggested. "Why don't the four of us—"

"Drew," A.W. interrupted, "could I speak with you a moment?"

"Uh, sure, Gramps."

Cassie looked to Grammy Jo for an explanation as the two men moved off into a huddle, but her grandmother pretended great interest in a nearby display of ballooning pins. Cassie watched Drew's expression go from shock to smiling delight in a matter of seconds. What was going on?

The two men returned, and A.W. took Grammy Jo by the hand again. "I guess we'll see you two later," he said with feigned nonchalance. He reminded Cassie of a sixteen-year-old who had just wangled the car keys and had things to do and people to see.

"You're leaving?"

"Yep," A.W. responded with a little grin. "So long."

"But—"

"Drew will explain," Grammy Jo said over her shoulder as they hurried toward the parking lot and A.W.'s green MG.

Cassie turned to Drew. "They're leaving, just like that? I figured they might make a date for tonight, but this is very sudden." She stared at Drew's amused expression. "What's so funny?"

"They do have a date for tonight."

"That's nice."

"Today, tonight and tomorrow."

Cassie's mouth dropped open. "As in continuously?"

"That's right. They're driving to Santa Fe to spend the rest of the weekend."

"But they don't have any extra clothes or toothbrushes or..." Cassie sputtered to a stop. She wasn't sure she approved of this at all.

His tone was tolerant. "They've thought of that. They'll stop by each house and pick up a few things before they leave."

"What if Grammy Jo forgets her blood-pressure medication?" Cassie wailed. "What if A.W. drives the car too fast? What if—"

"What if they have a terrific time?" Drew caught her shoulders and shook her gently. "Cassie, isn't this what you wanted?"

"It's all happening so fast." She narrowed her eyes at him. "Your grandfather is a fast mover, Drew Bennett. Just like you."

He burst out laughing. "Your grandmother suggested the trip, not A.W."

"Grammy Jo? Well, I suppose I shouldn't be surprised. She's never been an indecisive woman. I hope she's not doing this for me, that's all."

"Did you see the look in her eyes? I don't think she's doing this for you, Cassie."

"I guess not. I only thought— Well, she's been talking about getting out of my way so that— Maybe A.W. is a convenient method to..." She glanced down and rubbed the toe of her tennis shoe in the dirt.

Drew tilted her chin up. "They're going away together because they find each other exciting. It's that simple. As for the rest of it, yes, maybe you are a little more free, at least for the next twenty-four hours. And so am I. Except I'm a little strapped for transportation right now. Care to give me a lift home?" His brown eyes challenged her.

Her worries about Grammy Jo blunted her joy at the prospect of spending time alone with Drew. "Possibly."

"I could give you a tour of the house. You've never seen the whole thing, have you?"

"No," she said, playing along. "I guess I haven't."

He rubbed his thumb sensuously along her lower lip. "I'm sure I forgot to show you the master bedroom."

"That's true." Cassie tried to put aside her concern for Grammy Jo and concentrate on what Drew was saying. Wasn't this what she'd longed for, time to talk with Drew? And yes, time to love him, as well.

"Stay with me until tomorrow, Cassie," he said softly. "Their chance to be alone is ours, too."

"What if something goes wrong and she tries to reach me at home?"

"She'll know to call my house. But nothing will go wrong." He took a deep breath. "And I need you so much."

Cassie allowed the glow of desire in his dark eyes to persuade her. "I...I'll need to pick up a few things at the house, too."

Drew nodded. "We'd better approach the place with caution. It wouldn't do to run into our grandparents at this delicate point in their relationship."

"Oh, Drew, are you sure they'll be okay?"

"Yes." He took her hand, and they walked toward the parking lot.

When they arrived at Grammy Jo's, they saw no sign of A.W.'s car.

"I bet they've been and gone," Drew said as they entered the quiet house.

"Maybe. I feel so strange about all this. I'm going to check and make sure she took her medication."

Drew followed her into Grammy Jo's room. "And what if she didn't? Are we going to hightail it up to Santa Fe and check all the hotels until we find her?"

Cassie stopped, her hand midway to the drawer in the bedside table. "No." She turned to face him. "I'm not handling this situation very well, am I?"

"You're doing fine." Drew sensed the internal conflict in her as she wrestled with the idea of her grandmother's becoming involved with another man. He wanted to whisk her away to a day and night of lovemaking. It was what he needed, but what about Cassie? "I have an idea," he said. "Get your racquetball stuff."

She looked at him.

"Yeah, I mean it. We'll go to my place to change and then hit the courts."

The sparkle in her hazel eyes told him he'd come up with the perfect plan.

As she hurried to pack, he wandered into the living room, congratulating himself all the way. For once in dealing with Cassie he'd put his psychologist's training to good use. Usually when she was around, he forgot everything he'd ever been taught about human behavior and reacted with gut-level emotions. Did love do that, reduce people to a primitive "me Tarzan, you Jane" mind-set?

"Ready." She appeared beside him. "Here's your racquet."

"That's okay. I have one of my own now."

"You do? Well, let's take this one, anyway, in case your new one doesn't react quite the way you expect it to. Every racquet is different, you know."

"It reacts okay."

"You've tried it?"

"A few times. Come on, let's go."

They loaded Cassie's small suitcase and racquetball bag into the back seat of the Toyota. "What few times?" she said as she slid behind the wheel and started the car.

"Here and there," he answered casually as they drove away from the curb.

"You've been practicing! During those days between the trip to Phoenix and the party you've been practicing, haven't you?"

"A little. Had to find some way to work off my frustrations. A cute little gal with dimples suggested it. Said I had the body for it."

"You're pretty sneaky, practicing like crazy and then casually suggesting we play a few games."

He grinned. She was okay now. He would let her think he'd planned the racquetball if that was what it took to put that happy lilt back in her voice.

"And now you think you can whip the pants off me."

"Nifty expression, Cassie. I like it."

"You know what I meant," she retorted with a saucy flip of her head.

"I hope so." He winked at her. *Oh, Cassie, this is how I love to see you, spunky and full of fun, not weighed down with worry about your grandmother.*

"Well, Drew Bennett, you're in for a surprise if you think you can beat me that easily. You couldn't possibly learn in a few days what I've been perfecting for years. But I'll be glad to give you a shot."

"Confident little devil, aren't you?"

"About this, yes."

"That's good. I like cocky ladies. It'll be a shame to win and prove you wrong," he said, deliberately baiting her and watching with joy as her cheeks flushed in response to his challenge.

"You're a dreamer. I was easy on you before, but now I'm taking you to the cleaners, fella."

"We'll see."

LATER, AS HE RACED MADLY around the court, he wondered what kind of masochist he was, taunting her into this kind of display. She was a magnificent player, and he was likely to be a physical wreck before the morning was over. If they didn't stop soon, his other plans for their time together would be down the tubes.

His only consolation was that with each victory another layer of tension seemed to slip away from her. If he could hold out long enough, she'd be more than ready for a wonderful romp in his king-sized bed. Trouble was, he might be ready for the emergency room.

When he hit the concrete floor for the sixth time while diving for and missing a shot, he formed a T with the racquet and his free hand.

"Give?" she asked, sauntering over to where he sat panting.

"My biorhythms must be off today or something."

"Baloney. Admit you've had your behind whipped by a superior player, Bennett."

From his position on the floor, he had an enticing

view up the silky length of her thigh to the tender skin beneath the hem of her shorts. The part of him that had not been exercised stirred in response, but the rest of him felt like a wrung-out washcloth.

"Drew, you don't look so great."

"Thanks. You look fresh as a daisy."

She held out her hand. "Come on, let's get you home and into a warm shower."

He needed her support more than he wanted to admit as she helped him up. "I should be in better shape than this. After all, I do weight lifting."

"That doesn't help much with endurance or coordination." She handed him a towel to wipe his face.

"Are you calling me uncoordinated?"

She gave him the kind of smile that made him hope she was imagining their nights together. "No, I wouldn't say you're uncoordinated."

He limped through the door of the racquetball court. "That's good."

"This sport requires different kinds of moves, that's all."

"Oh." He wondered if he would have any moves left for later. Opening the passenger's side of her Toyota, he flopped onto the seat and laid his head back against the headrest.

Cassie drove carefully, occasionally glancing at Drew. His eyes were closed, and at a stoplight she studied his slumped form with tender concern. His ego had gotten him into this condition, but she felt sorry for him nevertheless. "Have you got any Ben-Gay at home?"

He chuckled. "The sweet smell of Ben-Gay. How romantic."

"I'll rub it on," she offered.

"Oh, yeah?" He opened one eye. "That sounds better."

Cassie hoped he wasn't too exhausted. The racquetball match had invigorated her, and just looking at Drew caused her skin to prickle with desire. Had she sabotaged his ability to make love to her?

When they arrived at his house, she ordered him into the shower immediately, and he didn't protest. "Do you have another bathroom besides yours?" she called after him.

"Second door to the right," he said over his shoulder. "I'll meet you in my bedroom in fifteen minutes."

"With the Ben-Gay," she prompted.

She found the guest bathroom and showered quickly. After drying herself on a large, fluffy towel, she debated what to put on. Nothing in her small suitcase seemed quite appropriate for the occasion. Clothes were too formal, and her negligee seemed silly in the middle of the day.

Finally, in a rush of bravery, she wrapped the towel around her breasts and tucked the ends in securely.

She tried to quell her excitement as she walked down the tiled hallway to Drew's bedroom. After all, he might ask for the rubdown and fall asleep immediately afterward. His muscles might not be ready for what she had in mind. But that was only if she allowed him to do most of the work. What if she became the aggressor? The idea warmed every inch of her already tingling skin.

He walked through his bathroom door into his bedroom at the same moment she came in. She smiled as she noticed the towel draped around his hips. He had made the same choice she had. And oh, he was gorgeous, this dark-haired man, his beard and chest hair glistening with captured drops of water from his shower.

He stopped and looked at her for a long time and then sighed. "If you've ruined me for loving you, Cassie Larue, I'm going to be very upset."

"You ruined yourself," she chided, "by bragging about your newfound skills and forcing me to teach you a lesson."

He held up a bottle of white liquid. "Let's see if I can be repaired."

Cassie ordered him to lie facedown on the bed first while she sat beside him and massaged the pungent lotion into his shoulder and back muscles. The menthol heated her kneading fingers while her thoughts fueled the warmth building inside her body.

He coughed. "God, that stuff is strong, Cassie."

"It's good for you." She dotted more lotion on her palm and worked it into his thigh and calf muscles. She longed to stray beneath the concealing towel, but she'd never finish her job if she did. "How does that feel?"

"Mmf."

"You're not going to sleep, are you?" She stopped her massage and bent to peer into his face. "Are you?"

She saw his eyelid twitch a split second before his arm snaked out and grabbed her, pulling her down on the bed as he rolled to his back.

"How can a man sleep when a sexy woman wearing only a scrap of terry cloth is rubbing her hands all over him?" He was working to remove both his towel and hers. Then he grimaced in pain. "Oh, Cassie, I'm a broken man."

"I doubt it," she crooned. "But you're working much too hard at this. Lie back and relax for a change. Leave the driving to me."

He raised both eyebrows. "Really?"

"Really."

9

CASSIE SLID OFF THE BED and padded into his bathroom.

"But you're leaving," he protested.

She turned on the faucet and washed her hands. "Ben-Gay is not the lotion for what I have in mind," she said, rummaging through his medicine cabinet. "Ah, this is better."

"Cassie, come here."

She stood in the doorway and flung away her towel. "You just lie still, Dr. Bennett, and stop issuing orders when you're in no condition to do so."

His hungry gaze roamed her uncovered body. "You're taking advantage of an injured man."

"I'm certainly going to try." Cassie returned to the bed with the small tube of moisturizing lotion in her hand. "I'm surprised you even have this. Most men don't."

"Free sample. My mail lady brought it."

Cassie smiled. "And little did she know, when she delivered that free sample, what a valuable bit of junk mail it was." She rubbed a bit of fragrant lotion between her palms and placed them on his chest. Slowly she rotated her hands, caressing his nipples and the springy hair on his chest.

"Thank God for junk mail," Drew said, watching her breasts bob in rhythm with her massage.

She paused for more lotion and moved lower, across

his flat stomach and down. The towel had slipped away, and when her hands found the hard shaft that announced his erection, he groaned with the pleasure of her touch.

She teased and stroked until his breathing became a harsh, rasping sound. At last he moaned her name and reached for her.

"No," she said, pushing his shoulders flat. "I'm in charge here."

"Then you'd better do something fast. I'm going crazy."

She eased her body above his and took him inside her, sighing as he filled the aching void that touching him had created. With arms braced on either side of his head, she rocked slowly, watching his eyes close at the intensity of the sensations she was arousing in him.

"Are you all right?" she whispered, wanting to be certain she wasn't hurting his overworked body.

His eyes opened, but they were glazed with passion. "A lot...more than...all right," he said, gasping. "Cassie, you...Cassie..." His jaw muscles clenched.

She bent to kiss his parted lips as she increased the tempo. He would be first, she decided. This time was for him. She felt his body tense as he tried to control his response to her sensual movements. Then, with a strangled cry, he abandoned the fight and thrust upward.

She took the force of his release joyfully, glad to know he was strong enough to let her lead, to let her see his vulnerability in the face of desperate need. Moments later she joined him with her own cry of completion. As her explosive reaction ebbed, Cassie seemed to be floating, drifting on a warm current of air, rocked to sleep in a wicker cradle held aloft by a silken rainbow.

WHEN NEXT SHE OPENED HER EYES, Cassie judged from the shadows on the wall that it was late afternoon. And she was starving. Drew still slept beside her, apparently more in need of rest than food. Cassie smiled, remembering the trouble his boast had gotten him into. He was liable to be very stiff when he awoke, despite the Ben-Gay.

She got out of bed quietly and crept out of the room in search of her clothes first and a snack second. She dressed in the guest bathroom, repinned her disheveled hair and headed for the kitchen.

She had to open several cupboards and search the contents of the refrigerator, but soon her arms were loaded with cheese, crackers, an apple and a large glass of milk, all of which she carted out through a sliding glass door to the back patio. She had finished the apple and half the cheese and crackers by the time Drew found her.

"You had me worried," he said, his expression relieved as he smiled down at her.

"Worried?"

"When I woke up and you were gone, I thought maybe I'd dreamed that you were here." He sat down beside her on the redwood chaise. "Oh, my aching bones."

"You smell like Ben-Gay."

"Some postal worker rubbed it all over me. Said she had experience handling the male, but I think she's confused about the spelling of the word."

Cassie choked on her milk. "I knew you'd work that pun in sooner or later."

"I waited as long as I could." He stretched one leg gingerly in front of him. "Ouch."

"The massage didn't help?"

"It was of great benefit to my libido, but I'm afraid it didn't cure my racquetball injuries."

"I shouldn't have run you so hard, but you were awfully pompous about your chances of winning."

He helped himself to a cracker and a slice of cheese. "I may need a little more practice before I can beat you."

"A little? Didn't this morning tell you anything? You can't just—" She stopped ranting when she realized he was grinning at her. "You're a big tease, Drew Bennett. That's what got you into trouble."

"It was worth it. I think I'll put you in charge more often."

Cassie smiled at him and marveled that she had ever found him intimidating. He was intelligent and sexy and funny, but not really intimidating. She felt brave enough to bring out the letter Evan had sent her and the copy of the handwriting sample.

"Stay here a minute," she said. "I have something to show you."

"I like how this is starting out."

"No, this has nothing to do with sex, so calm yourself."

"Aw, shucks."

"I'll be right back."

She returned to find him stretched out in the chaise, finishing the last of her glass of milk. "I see you made yourself right at home."

"This is my home."

"True, but I fixed that snack."

"In my kitchen with my food." His dark eyes laughed up at her.

"Consider it payment for services rendered."

He caught her hand and pulled her down next to him. "In that case, what would you do for a steak?"

She swept his supine body with a haughty gaze. "In your present disabled condition, you couldn't handle it."

His grip moved to her arm, and he brought her closer. "Try me."

Her senses responded immediately to his nearness. The familiar curve of his mustache and beard framing his sensuous mouth made her lips tingle in anticipation, just as his touch on her arm renewed the memory of his caress. "Don't kiss me," she murmured as his breath blended with hers.

His tone was lazy, sexy. "I know kissing's not original, but I like it."

"I want to talk to you."

"Let's use body language."

She grasped the folded papers firmly in her hand to remind herself of her mission. "Look at these first." She sat up with an effort and held out the letter.

"Can't you put it in a memo? Or better yet, leave it in my mailbox?"

"No."

"Stubborn, aren't you?" He took the paper and unfolded it. "This better be good, Larue. Hey, this is from Evan."

"It's about his client, the one who speaks Portuguese."

"Yes, I can see that." Drew read the letter quickly and looked up. "You're not really going to charge him, are you?"

Cassie was taken aback, and her instinctive response was defensive. "Why not? I performed a service."

"Well, then, maybe a few dollars."

"Sixty."

"Sixty bucks?"

"Drew, you have no idea how much work is involved in a complete analysis. Let me show you something." She shoved the handwriting sample forward.

"This is the man's writing?"

"Yes."

"Even I can tell he's a weirdo, Cassie, if he draws lines like that through all his letters."

"He didn't. I did. The slanted lines reveal his emotional response to situations. In this case, the slant leans to the right, which means a high response."

"Or he had the paper turned."

"No, that doesn't make a difference."

"I bet it does."

"No, Drew, not really," she insisted, trying to be patient. "Now look at his formation of the letter *o* and the letter *a*."

"Pretty good job. He must have had Miss Dolittle in third grade, like I did. Or her clone."

"You're right, his formation is like yours, but not because you had the same handwriting teacher. It's because you have the same personality trait of honesty, both with yourself and others."

"Hey, wait a minute. This guy's accused of killing someone. I'm not wild about being compared to him."

"That may be the only trait you have in common,

other than pride. He's a light line writer, which means he usually doesn't follow through on projects. Your writing indicates just the opposite. You're decisive and determined to finish what you start. This man doesn't have the force of character to commit murder."

"But I do? That's great to hear, Cassie."

She sighed. "That's not what I meant at all. In graphoanalysis we take all the traits together and come up with a picture of the whole person. I think this fellow is innocent, and I hope he's acquitted."

Drew stared at her. "On the basis of how he makes his *o*'s and *a*'s, you're ready for society to turn him loose?"

Cassie shifted uneasily on the chaise. The discussion wasn't going at all as she'd hoped. "Not just that. I gave you those formations as an example. I've spent hours on this sample, and I know far more about the man than what those two letters indicate. He's not a killer, not from what I see."

"That's fine. You're entitled to your opinion."

"My opinion is based on scientific study."

Drew sat up and swung his legs to the ground. "Now that's where we differ, I'm afraid. I believe that you spent hours studying this man's handwriting. I can't accept that your findings should be labeled scientific."

"That's a prejudiced viewpoint." Cassie began to realize the futility of her arguments. Heavy writers like Drew held on to their beliefs. "I was hoping you'd reconsider that stand."

He looked at her. "I wish I could. You're a warm, wonderful woman, Cassie, and I think you know how much you mean to me. But I won't pay lip service to this handwriting business to placate you and keep this relationship on an even keel."

She rose and gazed out across the stark New Mexico landscape, its barren beauty softened by the warm light from the setting sun. "Of course you won't. You're too honest. I know that about you, Drew. And I know how much you care for me because you're capable of deep emotions as well as strong prejudices. It's all in your handwriting."

He got to his feet with a muffled groan. "To hell with the handwriting. You don't need an analysis to figure out my feelings about you, Cassie. I've made them pretty damn obvious. The person who's not so obvious is you. How do you feel about me, Cassie? Do you care enough to tolerate my opinion, or are you willing to let this difference drive us apart?"

She faced him, tears shining in her eyes. "I'm not sure."

"Let me make you sure," he said softly, taking a step forward.

"No." She recoiled from his touch.

He stopped abruptly, a hard look in his eyes.

"I don't want this to be a meeting of bodies only," Cassie said, her voice strained by emotion. "That's not good enough, Drew."

"Don't give me that. We have more working for us than sex, and you know it. You're being melodramatic."

"I guess it's a trait I inherited from Grammy Jo. I'm going home, Drew."

"You are home."

"A couple of hours ago I would have agreed with you. Everything felt so right here. That's why I rummaged around in your kitchen without asking. I felt at home. But home is a place where dreams are nurtured, Drew. I don't think you'll be able to nurture mine."

She pushed past him and ran into the house to gather her belongings. When she had her suitcase, she glanced out to the patio. He stood with his back to her, staring into the red glare of the setting sun. With a sob she hurried through the house and out the front door to her car.

Drew listened to her drive away and swore eloquently. Then he marched into the house, picked up the telephone and called Evan Farber.

"You busy, Ev?" he asked when his friend answered.

"Just checking my ski equipment and praying for an early snow in the mountains. What's happening?"

"That's my line. I understand you're offering to pay Cassie for that handwriting stuff."

"I sure am. Her analysis was damn valuable. Wish I could use it in court, but at least I have a handle on the guy's personality and some ideas about how to verify it with other tests."

"Come on, Ev. You don't really believe her conclusions are valid, do you?"

Evan was silent for a moment. "Yes, but obviously you don't. I thought there was something going on between you two. Romantically speaking."

"There is—was. But she insists that I swallow this handwriting business hook, line and sinker. I'm having a lot of trouble with that."

"So I see."

"Today she showed me your letter offering to pay

her, and I had to find out if you were serious or just being polite."

"I was serious, and I think you'd better open that thick skull of yours a little, old buddy. Graphoanalysis might even help your practice."

Drew snorted. "Sure."

"Do you know anything about it?"

"I checked out some books from the library, but I couldn't get through the first one, and I took them back."

"Let me send you some material. I've considered taking the course myself."

"You?"

"Why not? But for now Cassie is way ahead of anything I could learn in the next few months. Her help could be a real asset to me."

Drew sighed. "I seem to be the one out of step here. Okay, if you'd be kind enough to send me something to read on the subject, I'll try to keep an open mind."

"Be glad to. Of course, you could probably get the same information from Cassie."

"I'd rather you sent it to me, Ev."

"Do I detect a little stubborn pride?"

"Probably. Just send me the stuff, okay?"

Evan laughed. "Sure."

CASSIE FELT EXTREMELY LUCKY that her racquetball buddy, Ruth, was available for a match Sunday morning. And Cassie apologized for her aggressive behavior in beating Ruth soundly in every game. Afterward they talked about Grammy Jo's new romance and carefully avoided any mention of what was happening with Cassie's love life.

She was in the shower when Grammy Jo returned from Santa Fe. By the time she was out and wrapped in a bathrobe, A.W. had gone and Grammy Jo was unpacking in her bedroom. Her happy humming told Cassie most of what she wanted to know.

Swallowing her own misery, she adopted a cheerful expression and sauntered into Grammy Jo's room. "Have a nice time?"

"You might say that." Grammy Jo looked as if she could stand in the corner and double as a floor lamp, her face was so bright with happiness.

"No big fights?"

"He admitted that Robert Redford made him feel inferior," Grammy Jo said with a smile. "But after this weekend I don't have that much of a hankering for Robert Redford somehow."

Cassie crossed to her grandmother and gave her a hug. "I'm so happy for you."

"I'm happy for both of us, you with your psychologist and me with my surgeon. How was your weekend without the two old fuddy-duddies around to spy on you?"

"Oh..." Cassie was about to tell Grammy Jo about her problems with Drew, but then she saw the look of eager anticipation on Grammy Jo's face. "It was nice," she said with a wink.

"Maybe the four of us should do something special," Grammy Jo said, her expression animated. "I'll treat. What do you think? Dinner at High Finance? A.W. said he'd never been on the Tramway at night."

"Why, uh, sure, I guess we could," Cassie stammered. What now? An evening with Drew with them pretending affection for each other? Maybe he wouldn't agree to go. But he would if she asked him, she realized. He wasn't the kind of man to put her in an uncomfortable position.

"Let's see. A.W. and I will be busy with the Balloon Fiesta for the next few days, but our evenings will be free. Well, some of them. Tonight we're going to the movies, and tomorrow night's a concert." Grammy Jo bustled around putting her clothes and cosmetics in their proper places. "How about Tuesday night? Will you check with Drew?"

"Of course."

Grammy Jo paused in her unpacking to beam at Cassie. "Ain't love grand?"

Cassie nodded while inside her a voice screamed that love wasn't grand at all. It was the source of the worst pain she'd ever known, and she'd be so grateful to have never met a man who could hurt her the way Drew was doing.

LATER THAT EVENING, after Grammy Jo and A.W. had left for the movies, Cassie dialed Drew's number. When he answered, she couldn't speak right away.

"Cassie, is that you?"

"Yes," she managed.

"You sound terrible. Are you sick?"

"No."

"I feel as if I've got the flu, but I know it's from racquetball." He was silent, obviously waiting for her to say why she'd called.

"Drew, I still feel the same way I did yesterday, but—"

"When yesterday? BS or AS?"

"What?"

"Before Snack or After Snack."

"Drew, this is serious."

"I know." His voice grew more intense. "Cassie, don't do this to us."

"This call is not about us at all, really. It's about A.W. and Grammy Jo. Did you tell your grandfather about our little...disagreement?"

"No."

"That's good because I didn't tell Grammy Jo. I couldn't spoil her euphoria today. Consequently she thinks we're still—"

"I am."

Cassie's hand, gripping the phone, began to shake. "She...she wants us all to have dinner together Tuesday night at High Finance," she rushed on. "Her treat."

"A.W. will never let her do that."

"Will you go?"

"You know I will, Cassie."

"Fine. A.W. will have the details. Goodbye, Drew." She hung up quickly before the receiver could drop from her trembling hand. Then she took out her typewriter and began pounding out her bill for Evan. On the table beside her was the handwriting sample that she had hoped would convince Drew of her professionalism. She picked up the page and examined it once more. The characters blurred as the paper absorbed her quiet tears.

GRAMMY JO HAD RESERVED a table next to the window overlooking the rhinestone-on-black-velvet city far below them. The restaurant, at the top of the Tramway that ran up Sandia Peak, boasted Albuquerque's most famous view. But Cassie noticed that her grandmother didn't spend much time admiring it. Her attention was captivated by the gray-haired man seated next to her. They held hands on top of the table and constantly exchanged lovers' glances. Cassie was envious.

The two couples sat across from each other at the rectangular table. The window with its spangled view was on Cassie's left, and Drew was uncomfortably close on her right. If she shifted in her seat, she was in danger of brushing her knee against his. Occasionally their arms bumped when he reached for his wine or she for her knife. She suspected his knee was closer than necessary, his arm slightly past his half of the table.

After one collision he glanced at her and smiled innocently. "I'm not crowding you, am I?"

She returned his smile and then lowered her voice so that A.W. and Grammy Jo wouldn't hear. "I guess you need space for such a large ego."

"Ouch. The lady fights rough."

"She has to," Cassie murmured before responding to A.W.'s question about junk mail. "Actually, we don't deliver everything we get," she said. "If we did, your mailbox would be a lot more stuffed than it is."

"Cassie's discriminating about what she delivers," Drew added. When she kicked him under the table, he didn't even wince. "I only get the good junk. Just the other day she brought me a tube of hand lotion. I can't tell you how useful that's been."

"The fact is," Cassie said with a breathtaking smile at Drew, "some people like getting junk mail. Now that I know how much Drew appreciates his, I plan to see that he gets a lot more to open."

"Oh, goody."

Grammy Jo glanced reprovingly at her granddaughter. "Stop that teasing, Cassie. I swear you never let that poor boy rest."

Drew nodded. "She does have a smart mouth on her, Grammy Jo. But I like my woman to have a little spunk. Keeps me on my toes."

Cassie gasped. "*Your* woman?"

"Children, children." A.W. clinked his fork against his glass. "Stop squabbling. Someday you'll realize how foolish that is. When you've reached Jo's and my age, you understand that it's better to be a lover than a fighter."

Cassie almost choked on her wine. This from a man who was willing to allow an argument about Robert Redford end his chances to court Grammy Jo?

"You're so right, A.W. Disputes over trivial matters are so ridiculous," Jo said, squeezing his hand.

Cassie glanced from one to the other in amazement. Didn't their memories extend back a week? Without her and Drew's interference, A.W. and Grammy Jo wouldn't be sitting here together, and all because of a silly disagreement that shouldn't have mattered to anyone. Some gratitude!

"The problem is," Drew said, laying down his fork, "that each of us has a different definition of trivial."

Cassie stiffened. Would he air their conflict in front of their grandparents and enlist their support on his side? She turned to him in supplication. "Drew, please...."

"But Cassie and I are working to bring ours into line with each other's," he finished, taking her hand in his. "In spite of the supposed squabbling you see, I love her very much." His gaze searched hers, telling her silently that his words were not a prepared speech made for the benefit of their dinner companions.

Cassie reeled from the shock of hearing Drew say for the first time that he loved her, in the middle of a crowded restaurant and in the company of A.W. and Grammy Jo. She opened her mouth to speak, but nothing came out.

"We can see that," Grammy Jo said happily, "and that's why I thought we should all be together tonight."

Cassie wondered why her own paralyzed reaction to Drew's statement wasn't mirrored in A.W. and Grammy Jo until she realized that the older couple had no reason to think this was the first occasion that Drew had proclaimed his feelings for her.

"Yes, indeed," A.W. said. "In fact, Jo and I have no objection to a double ceremony, if you kids would like that. Of course, maybe you want your own wedding. We can understand that, too."

Cassie blinked and tore her gaze from Drew's. "Wedding?" she croaked. "What wedding?"

Grammy Jo smiled across the table at her granddaughter. "A.W. and I are getting married, Cassie. Just as soon as he can clear up a few things in Phoenix."

10

"BUT YOU HARDLY KNOW each other!" Cassie protested.

"Ah, you're wrong," Grammy Jo said. "We know each other very well. We've lived long enough to figure out how to cut through the garbage and get on with things. And we're very compatible, both in bed and out."

Cassie flushed. "Grammy Jo!"

Drew squeezed Cassie's hand, which he'd continued to hold firmly during the revelation of the older couple's wedding plans. "I think it's great. Congratulations, both of you."

Cassie worked to recover her poise. "I think it's wonderful, too, Grammy Jo. And A.W." She smiled at the older man. "You caught me by surprise, that's all. Somehow I expected this process to take more time."

"We don't need more time, Cassie," A.W. said. "And Lord knows we don't have a lot of time to waste, no matter how young we feel right now."

Drew rubbed Cassie's thumb with his own. "Have you set a date?"

"Not yet," Grammy Jo replied. "We wanted to talk with both of you first." She paused and glanced from Cassie to Drew. "In case you two might—"

"No," Cassie said abruptly. "Drew and I have no immediate plans like that." She felt Drew's fingers tighten around hers and wanted to pull away, but the movement would have been too obvious in front of Grammy Jo and A.W.

"Then I guess we'd better decide which day, Jo," A.W. said. He glanced mischievously at his bride-to-be. "What do you think of Halloween?"

Grammy Jo chuckled. "I think it sounds just like you, and I'd love it. We'll have jack-o'-lanterns all round and a scarecrow or two. I know! We'll have all the guests come in costume."

Drew groaned and passed his hand over his face.

"Great idea, Jo. Where shall we hold it?"

"Well," Grammy Jo began, "there's a nice little church over on—"

"I think—" Drew cleared the laughter from his throat "—I think maybe you'd better have it at my place. Sounds like it may be a bit rowdy for a church."

"Maybe so," Grammy Jo conceded.

"Just maybe," Cassie added with a grin.

"So," Drew continued, "do you have honeymoon plans, or will you use the trip back to Phoenix as a honeymoon?"

"Oh, we aren't going back to Phoenix," Grammy Jo said.

"You're not? I figured you and Gramps would live there."

"Well, no, we're planning to live in my house, Drew. That way all four of us can be together in the same town. Won't that be more fun?"

"Why, sure. Sure it will. I suppose you'll sell the house, then, Gramps?"

A.W. nodded.

For the first time Cassie realized how complicated the situation was becoming. In less than a month

Grammy Jo would bring a new husband into the house she'd been sharing with Cassie. In addition, the two grandparents confidently assumed that she and Drew were serious about each other and would eventually marry.

Grammy Jo noticed Cassie's silence. "Don't worry, sweetheart. I'm not planning to kick you out. You're free to stay until you and Drew...as long as you like."

"Oh, no, I couldn't hang around and interfere with you two lovebirds," Cassie said, trying to sound light-hearted. "I'll find a small apartment."

"She's welcome to stay with me," Drew said, "but you know Cassie—an old-fashioned girl."

A.W. chuckled. "From the look in your eye, Drew, I doubt Cassie will live in that apartment long. If you two change your minds about a double ceremony, just holler."

"Don't push them, A.W." Grammy Jo nudged him. "Maybe they want their own chance to be in the spotlight. And perhaps they don't want to get married on Halloween."

"Don't know why not," A.W. replied. "The concept really appeals to me. The ultimate trick or treat."

"Oh, really? Better watch your sassy mouth, you old rascal. You haven't got me yet."

"I think I have." He kissed her hand.

Grammy Jo sighed. "You're right. You have."

"You know," A.W. continued, "this wedding could be great. I think we should be in costume, too."

"Why not?" Grammy Jo agreed. "Who needs those fancy tuxedos and long gowns that cost a million dollars? A.W., this is going to be a blast."

Cassie watched them wistfully. They were good for

each other, both feisty enough to appreciate each other's sense of humor and enthusiasm for life. She and Drew behaved like that when they were together until they came up against the one subject they couldn't discuss.

"And we want Cassie to be the maid of honor and Drew the best man," Grammy Jo added.

"In costume, of course," Drew said.

"Absolutely," Grammy Jo replied. "Don't worry. I'll help you figure out what to be. I owe you both that much. Without you two we wouldn't have met."

"The first and second time," Drew pointed out.

Grammy Jo and A.W. exchanged a long look.

"We almost blew it," A.W. admitted. "I'm glad you and Cassie were persistent."

"The credit really goes to Cassie," Drew said and turned to her. "Can I tell them about the box and the retirement magazine?"

"I guess so. Now that everything's turned out so well." Almost everything, she amended to herself. As Drew related Cassie's scheme, she noticed he left out any reference to handwriting analysis. Once again he was ignoring her ability in that area. Her thoughts returned to his public declaration of love. Did he really love her? How could he and maintain his prejudiced position?

"But just think," A.W. said when the story was finished, "if it had been me living in the house instead of Drew, I probably would have met Jo, but you two young people might not have gotten together."

Drew raised Cassie's hand to his lips. "I know," he said, brushing her knuckles with a soft kiss. "Or if the magazine subscription department hadn't goofed up,

Cassie wouldn't have targeted me for that fake package. I've thought of calling the magazine and thanking them for their inefficiency."

"Let's invite the editor to the wedding!" Grammy Jo suggested. "Say, A.W., how would you like to see me on the cover of *Inspired Retirement*?"

A.W. beamed at her. "I've always thought you had cover-girl potential."

Drew looked bemused. "This will be a wedding to end all weddings."

"Don't forget to invite all your jailbird friends," A.W. said. "They're a great bunch."

"And I'm inviting all the ladies in my aerobics class," Grammy Jo said, "and Cassie can include the post-office people."

"One of my clients just finished doing time for mail fraud," Drew commented. "He'll get along great with them."

"And the relatives from both sides," A.W. said. "But they have to wear costumes, too. You know, Drew, I'll bet your father hasn't dressed up for Halloween since he was ten."

Cassie rolled her eyes. "Don't you think we'd better invite a ringmaster? This is sounding more and more like a circus." She wondered if her own parents would even come, let alone appear in costume. She doubted they'd make it.

"It'll be fun," A.W. insisted. "I propose a toast. To craziness and love. They go well together."

Still caressing Cassie's cold fingers, Drew reached over and picked up his wineglass with his free hand. "To craziness and love," he said as the four of them touched glasses.

As he drank, he held her gaze over the rim of his goblet. She couldn't turn away. Despite the problems between them, he still had the power to make her ache for him. And she was aching now.

When the check arrived, Grammy Jo insisted on paying for the meal. To Cassie's amazement A.W. allowed her to do it.

They rode the tram down the mountain and piled into Drew's Audi. Then they all fell silent as each of them realized they'd made no arrangements for how the evening would end.

Cassie knew that if she didn't speak up, someone might suggest that the older couple be dropped off at Grammy Jo's, and she and Drew could conveniently go on to his house. Three of the people in the car would appreciate that arrangement.

"I hate to be a party pooper, but I need to get some sleep," she said into the silence.

"Why, of course, sweetheart," Grammy Jo said. "If you'll just run us home, Drew, you and A.W. can go back to your house."

"I guess we have to consider the working girl among us," Drew said with a trace of sarcasm. "Some workdays must be rougher than others."

Cassie knew he was referring to last week when she had blithely given up her sleep to be with him. "Every week is different," she said, returning his challenging stare. "Besides, I anticipate a lot of junk mail tomorrow."

Drew shook his head ruefully and started the car. "And I think I know who's going to get most of it."

WHEN CASSIE OPENED Drew's mailbox the next morning and found a single red rose inside, she almost regretted stuffing the bundles of printed circulars and charity solicitations into it. Almost. A rose wasn't an apology, was it? A rose wasn't respect and understanding.

The stem was secured in a tiny vial of water, and it stayed fresh all day clipped to her vehicle's sun visor. The aroma filled the tiny Jeep, and several times she thought of throwing it away because the fragrance kept Drew solidly at the forefront of her mind.

But he probably would have been there, anyway, she decided. Why couldn't he be more like Evan, who was willing to believe there was validity in her work? Cassie knew the answer because she'd analyzed Evan's signature. The pressure of his stroke was lighter than Drew's. He wasn't as likely to cling to a prejudiced viewpoint. Yet she'd probably never fall in love with a man like Evan, whose emotional depth didn't begin to equal Drew's.

Cassie had to face the irony of her situation. Drew's greatest attraction for her, his depth of feeling, contributed to their biggest problem. He had formed a definite opinion about handwriting analysis, and Drew Bennett didn't change his mind easily.

Every day Drew's mailbox contained a single rose, and every day she took the flower and left as much junk mail as the box would hold. She knew it was a silly, childish thing to do, but it was at least a form of silent communication, the only communication she had.

A.W. left for Phoenix to settle his affairs. He was due back three days before Halloween. Grammy Jo decided to redecorate the house for his return so that he wouldn't feel as if he were living in the midst of her late husband's surroundings. Fortunately, the project left Grammy Jo too busy to notice Cassie's lack of contact with Drew.

Cassie filled her spare time playing vigorous games of racquetball with her friend Ruth and hunting for an apartment. She put off planning her costume for the wedding, afraid that Grammy Jo would want to coordinate the outfits for the maid of honor and the best man.

But when the wedding was only two weeks away, she decided that the design of her costume, and Drew's if necessary, had to be determined soon. She walked into the house after work and found Grammy Jo reading her daily letter from A.W.

Grammy Jo looked up when she heard Cassie's footsteps. "Another rose from Drew? Such a romantic fellow."

"And another letter from A.W.," Cassie rejoined. "He hasn't missed a day, has he?"

"No." Grammy Jo folded the letter quickly and stuffed it into the envelope.

Cassie smiled. "Must be pretty juicy if you're putting it away so fast."

"I told you that A.W. is a very virile man," Grammy Jo said with a girlish toss of her head.

"I'm surprised he doesn't call you, though. Wouldn't it be more exciting to talk to each other on the telephone?"

"Maybe that's what he's afraid of. At our age we can only take so much excitement, you know."

"Oh, sure. Tell me another one. You are the same two people who traipsed off in a hot-air balloon, the same two who are planning a Halloween wedding where everyone arrives in costume, the same two who decided to get married within a week of meeting, the same—"

"All right," Grammy Jo said, laughing. "Maybe letters are more romantic. I can keep them and read them as many times as I like. I'd feel funny tape-recording a conversation and playing that back a million times."

"Well, letters sure are cheaper."

"I suppose."

Cassie thought again about the restaurant bill that A.W. had allowed Grammy Jo to pay. And now he wasn't springing for any phone calls, either. And they were planning to live in Grammy Jo's house, not A.W.'s. Who would get the money from the sale of his house? Would it be shared?

"The new carpet looks super, Grammy Jo."

"Do you think A.W. will like it? I've sent him samples of it and the drapery material. He seemed pleased, but everything looks different when you see a whole room instead of a little piece of something."

"Is he, ah, helping you pay for any of this?"

"Heavens, no! It was my idea. He swore that living in the house the way it was when your grandfather died wouldn't bother him, but I don't think he understands the subtleties of it. Besides, I was sick of the same old stuff. I deserve a new color scheme to go along with a new husband, don't you think?"

"Sure you do, Grammy Jo." Cassie smiled reassuringly at her while privately wondering why A.W. wouldn't offer to pay for the redecorating. Or even to buy a new house in Albuquerque, if that's where they both wanted to live. Cassie had thought she understood what kind of person her grandmother was marrying, but lately A.W. hadn't been conforming to Cassie's image of him.

Dismissing her negative thoughts, Cassie returned to the topic that had to be discussed. "It's time to decide what I'm going to wear to the wedding," she said. "Have you figured out what you and A.W. will dress as?"

"We've elected to surprise each other, and I think it would be fun if you and Drew did the same thing, don't you? If he needs help with his costume, have him call me, but tell him to keep it a secret from you. That should add some zip to the ceremony."

"As if the ceremony needs any more zip."

"Did I tell you the minister agreed to dress up, too? I believe he plans to be Donald Duck."

"Grammy Jo, this wedding is going to be outrageous."

"That's the idea. So what do you want to be?"

Cassie didn't have to think long. "A World War I flying ace."

Grammy Jo clapped her hands. "Marvelous, marvelous. I know right where I can get one of those leather jackets. The leather helmet might be hard to find, but we can make one if we have to. And goggles. We'll have to find goggles and a scarf. You'll look adorable."

"What about you? Have you picked a costume?"

"Yes. I'm trying a little experiment to see if A.W. was listening. One day we were talking about our secret wishes, and I said mine was to play the part of either Chip or Dale, those little chipmunks at Disneyland. I said the problem was I needed a partner to be the other chipmunk."

"So you're going to be a chipmunk and see if he shows up as the other one."

"Yep."

"What if he doesn't?"

"Oh, it won't matter. But I think he will. Won't it be exciting to see if he does?"

"Grammy Jo, I've concluded that you thrive on uncertainty."

Her grandmother looked pleased. "I do like to live on the edge."

IN HER ROOM THAT NIGHT Cassie thought again about A.W. and his apparent change in character. She could understand the letters. They were romantic. But wouldn't a man like A.W. also call and say to hell with the long-distance charges? It was nice that he wrote letters, though. Some men would slit their wrists before committing their love to paper.

The letters! Why hadn't she considered them before? She had ample evidence of A.W.'s character in those letters, just waiting to be analyzed.

Cassie tried to picture herself asking Grammy Jo for one of them in order to study A.W.'s handwriting. *How would you like a special wedding present, Grammy Jo? I'll tell you all the personality traits, good and bad, of your beloved.* Nope. Cassie couldn't ask her grandmother for one of the letters. Grammy Jo had been very protective of their contents, anyway. She wouldn't appreciate Cassie's interest.

So what did she plan to do, slip one of the letters out of her grandmother's room, analyze it and put it back? Even if she pulled off such a stunt, how would she feel about herself afterward?

But Grammy Jo's future happiness might be at stake. Which was more important, personal integrity or her grandmother's happiness? After all, Cassie argued with herself, Grammy Jo wouldn't have met A.W. without her interference.

Finally Cassie put the problem before her friend Ruth while they rested after a racquetball match.

"I don't have anyone else to consult, Ruth. Obviously I can't ask Drew what he thinks of spying on A.W.'s correspondence. What should I do?"

"What exactly do you hope to learn from this analysis?"

"When A.W. was with Drew and me in Phoenix, he put on a show of being financially well-off. But now he's not acting like that at all. There's inconsistency there, maybe even duplicity, for all I know. I can tell from his handwriting if he's capable of monkeying with the truth or not."

"Okay, sounds reasonable." Ruth nodded. "Why can't you look at one of the envelopes before your grandmother opens her mail? Seems to me that's how you got a bead on Dr. Drew Bennett, from the envelopes he addressed."

"That's a great idea, but Grammy Jo always gets the mail before I come home. And lately, because she knows there will be a letter from A.W., she times her whole day around the mail delivery."

"It *is* weird that A.W. writes all the time instead of calling once in a while. But he must be well-off. Doesn't he have a big house in Phoenix?"

"He's supposed to, but I've never seen it. Drew has. That time Drew and I went over there, A.W. said he was having the place sprayed for crickets, remember?"

"Oh, yeah."

"And Grammy Jo thought it was an excuse, that A.W. was spending the night with some woman and didn't want to tell us that he'd rather be with her than entertain his grandson."

Ruth flipped her racquet around in one hand and thought. "Do you know his address? I've been to Phoenix a couple of times. I might be able to tell you if the house is in a ritzy area or not."

"Let me think. I take Grammy Jo's letters for her every morning. You know something? The address is a post-office box."

"Well, lots of people have those."

"You're right. And I'm probably imagining things. Furthermore, I can't steal one of A.W.'s letters out of Grammy Jo's room. That's dishonest."

Ruth flipped her racquet some more. "Maybe you don't have to."

"What do you mean?"

"Does A.W. know you're a graphoanalyst?"

"Not likely. Drew keeps my little 'hobby,' as he calls it, under wraps. I think he'd prefer that nobody found out what I do in my spare time besides play racquet-ball."

"I must admit he's acting like a turkey about this, Cassie."

"I must admit it, too. Anyway, what were you about to suggest?"

"I have the most brilliant idea. It's so brilliant that I may require you to let me win ten racquetball games in a row in exchange."

"Which is? Come on, Ruth."

"You don't have to steal a letter from your grandmother if you have one of your own."

Cassie's mouth dropped open. "Of course," she whispered. "All I have to do is write A.W. a letter myself."

"And then analyze his reply." Ruth smiled triumphantly. "Do I get my ten games?"

"That wouldn't really make you happy. You'd have to win fair and square to feel good about it."

"Dammit, Cassie, I should never have let you analyze my handwriting. You know too much. Okay, what do I get?"

"The satisfaction of helping a friend. And an invitation to go apartment hunting with me again tomorrow."

Ruth groaned. "Why don't you just move in with me?"

"You already have a roommate, and besides, we'd kill each other within a week. You're right. I do know you too well. And myself. I have a haphazard attitude toward meals, you like to eat on the dot. I usually stay up late, you're in bed by ten. We'd never make it, Ruth."

"Too bad about Drew. His personality suits you perfectly."

"Yeah, too bad. Well, I've got to run. I have a letter to compose. One that asks plenty of questions and definitely requires an answer."

Cassie mailed her letter the next day and waited anxiously for a reply. When it came four days later, she picked it up with shaking hands.

Grammy Jo stood at the kitchen counter stirring some instant soup for her dinner. "I confess I'm extremely curious about that letter," she said, glancing at her granddaughter.

"I asked him for a few suggestions for a wedding gift," Cassie answered honestly. "I wanted my present to be a surprise for you, at least. So I'm afraid I can't share my letter, either."

"Tease."

"Excuse me, Grammy Jo," Cassie said, trying to disguise her eagerness. "I'm going to read this in private." She hurried to her room, closed the door and took out her graphoanalysis supplies.

11

SLOWLY A.W.'S PERSONALITY PROFILE emerged under Cassie's scrutiny of the letter. She saw much that was encouraging, much that was similar to Drew's profile, in fact. A.W.'s pressure was firm; he was capable of loving Grammy Jo deeply. His lowercase *m*'s and *n*'s revealed an exploratory mind.

His *t* bars fairly flew across the page, and Cassie smiled at that evidence of his passion for life, the dashing optimism that had endeared him to Grammy Jo. But she couldn't ignore the definite bottom loops in his uppercase *m* and *n* formations. A.W. was worried about something. Very worried.

Cassie added that knowledge to one more trait that appeared again and again. The primary difference between A.W.'s handwriting and Drew's was the way they wrote their circular letters—*a, o, d* and *g*. Drew's were open, free of loops, demonstrating that his honesty, both with himself and others was strong. A.W.'s script, with interior loops on both sides of the circles, showed a tendency to rationalize his mistakes and to be secretive about his true situation.

As she poured over A.W.'s letter, Cassie grew increasingly uneasy. She had a compelling desire to know that he did, indeed, have a lovely home in Phoenix and an ample retirement income. Could he possibly be after Grammy Jo for her money?

Drew had seen the house. How long ago? Had he traded in the Cadillac because he really wanted a smaller car, or was the MG cheaper to drive? When she thought about the car, she remembered the chipped paint, the worn seat covers. Maybe an old MG was easier to obtain than a new luxury car.

Cassie's hand hovered over the telephone as she debated calling the only person besides A.W. himself who could answer her questions. Finally she dialed Drew's number.

He answered at once, and her pulse quickened right on schedule at the sound of his voice.

"Hello, Drew. I need to talk to you."

"Don't tell me the flower-in-the-mailbox routine finally worked."

"No. I mean, the roses have been lovely, but that isn't why— Could I come over? Right away?"

"Be my guest. I'm here sorting my junk mail. Takes a lot of my time lately."

"Oh."

"What, no snappy comeback? You must be very upset about something."

"I am."

"I hope you're a good kind of upset, Cassie. I've been waiting for this phone call for days."

"I'm not coming to discuss us," Cassie said flatly. "It's about A.W. and Grammy Jo."

"Oh." He sighed. "Okay. I'll be here. Want some dinner? I was about to fix something."

"I could come later."

"Dammit, Cassie! Can't you even have a hamburger with me? Are things that bad?"

"No, no, I guess not. I'll be right there."

HALF AN HOUR LATER she was sitting at Drew's kitchen table eating the hamburger and potato-chip meal that he served with a glass of wine for each of them. She hadn't explained the reason for her visit yet, and he seemed willing to make idle conversation instead.

Cassie admitted to herself that she was having a good time. Drew was excellent company, and she'd missed his sense of humor, his easy laugh. She'd forgotten about his little habit of rubbing his knuckles across his dark beard, and how his understanding gaze could make her feel warm and protected.

She missed lots of other things about him, too, but she couldn't allow herself to think about those, not when she had to concentrate on her original mission.

"More wine?" Drew got up to take the bottle out of the refrigerator. He wondered if the time was right to broach the subject of handwriting analysis. He'd begun reading the material Evan had sent by courier, and he had some questions.

"Half a glass. I have to drive home, you know."

"Not as far as I'm concerned." Could he convince her to stay the night? A picture of Cassie, her unclothed body rosy from the friction of his touch, flashed across his mind. Maybe they could leave the discussion of handwriting until later. Much later.

"I don't think I should stay." Her voice was low.

"Why not?" he asked gently.

She waved one hand in the air. "I just don't. I came over to ask you a few things about A.W."

"So ask them. Then we can settle the other matter." He filled her glass half full, as she'd requested, and his nearly to the brim.

Cassie folded her napkin and put it beside her plate,

stalling. Finally she began. "Can you imagine what A.W. might be worried about these days?"

"What makes you think he's worried?"

"I... A hunch." Cassie felt like a coward.

"He's making a major change in his life. That might worry him some. But he seems really happy about the marriage."

Cassie had to agree. She didn't believe A.W.'s worries had anything to do with his marriage to Grammy Jo. "How long has he lived in his house?"

"Oh, I don't know. He and my grandmother bought it when I was a teenager, so what's that—fifteen years or so? Why, do you think he's anxious about selling it?"

"Maybe." Cassie kept fishing. "Has he always had a post-office box?"

"No, he got it this year." Drew frowned impatiently. "Do I get to find out what's on your mind, or are we going to play twenty questions all evening?"

"All right." Cassie took a deep breath. "I have this crazy idea he's not living in that house anymore. That he sold it or...something several months ago and has been embarrassed to tell you."

"That's the silliest thing I've ever heard. Even if he did get rid of the house, to buy a condo maybe, he wouldn't be afraid to tell me about it."

"That depends on the circumstances of the sale."

Drew shoved his chair back. "I can't imagine what circumstances. Besides, Gramps went back to Phoenix to settle his affairs, which means specifically to sell the house."

"Not necessarily, Drew."

"What reason could you possibly have for doubting

it? Not to mention the fact that I'm really ticked off that you *are* doubting it. I don't care for your insinuations that he's not being truthful with us."

"Please don't get angry. You're the only one I can talk to about this. I realize it sounds awful to say such things, but the exterminator story wasn't very plausible, Drew."

"So he had a girlfriend to see that night. So what?"

"Why did he switch to a post-office address?"

"Maybe his mail carrier wasn't as cute as you. How do I know? People do that all the time."

"Have you been in the house since he got the post-office box?"

"No, but—"

"And think about it. Wasn't the Cadillac worth more than that old, beat-up MG?"

"He said he wanted to fix it up. Everyone needs a hobby."

"And they're going to live in Grammy Jo's house, not his."

"Now that has the most logical explanation of all, Cassie. They want to live in Albuquerque to be near us. Frankly, I think they expect to have fun spoiling their great-grandchildren in the future."

She turned away from his deliberate gaze. "Then I guess they'll be disappointed."

"Cassie..." Drew groaned. "How can I want to throttle you and kiss you at the same time?"

She stared silently at her plate.

"I don't want to fight," he continued, a note of pleading in his voice. "Not about Gramps. Not about anything."

Somewhere she found the courage to look at him. "Neither do I."

"Then...Cassie...I meant what I said in the restaurant."

She shook her head. "I don't think so. Or maybe we have different definitions of the word love."

"I'll give you mine. I want you near me every minute. I dream of holding you, loving you."

"That's sexual attraction, Drew."

"All right. Maybe it is, but I haven't touched you all evening. We've laughed and talked like old friends. Put that together with your sexual attraction, and what do you have?"

"Friends who are sexually attracted to each other."

"What I feel for you is far more intense than that, and you know it."

"There's something missing."

His tone hardened. "Yes, Cassie, and I'll tell you what it is. Commitment on both sides. Once again I've laid myself on the line, and you haven't. You haven't said how you feel about me."

"Drew, I—"

"We could approach this from the opposite angle. Can you tell me you don't love me?"

She folded her hands in her lap to keep them from shaking.

"Well, can you? That would straighten this out right quick. I'd know that I loved you but you didn't love me back. It happens. I can give you up or keep trying, but at least I'd know the score. So say it, Cassie. Say you don't love me."

"I didn't come here to talk about that," she said as

panic rose in her. "I came because I'm worried that A.W.'s financial situation isn't what we think it is."

"Why, in heaven's name? You haven't presented one point strong enough to make that statement."

"That's because I don't dare," she said quietly, pulling A.W.'s letter from her purse. "You won't credit my biggest piece of evidence."

"God," he whispered, staring at the paper, "you've analyzed his handwriting."

"Yes, and he's capable of deceiving both himself and others."

"Oh, is he? According to what, your crazy mumbo jumbo? Fat chance I'm going to believe that!" Drew stood and pointed a finger at her. "I bet you tricked him into writing to you, and then you raked him over the coals with your so-called scientific analysis. What does that reveal about your personality, Cassie?"

"I don't feel good about doing that," Cassie said, heat rising in her cheeks. "But I owe Grammy Jo something. Without me she wouldn't have met your grandfather. What if he's after her money?"

"What?" Drew shouted. "That's the most ludicrous thing I've ever heard, Cassie Larue! If you were someone else, I'd throw you bodily out of this house for that accusation."

She stood to face him. "I should have known I couldn't talk to you about this. You don't accept the scholarship of my study, and you're totally blind where your precious grandfather is concerned!" She grabbed her purse and marched to the front door. "Well, I have an obligation to Grammy Jo, and I'm damn well going to honor it!" She jerked the door open and slammed it behind her.

ANGER SUSTAINED HER for the next twelve hours, which was fortunate because she couldn't sleep. After several calls once she'd returned home, she found someone to substitute on her route the next day.

Grammy Jo had aerobics early in the morning and planned a day of furniture shopping, so Cassie had no trouble slipping out of the house in something other than her uniform. She drove to the Albuquerque airport and was soon on board a commuter plane bound for Phoenix.

She telephoned A.W. from the airport. "I'm taking a taxi out to your house," she said after dispensing with both the preliminary greetings and A.W.'s surprise that she was in town alone. "Can you give me directions?"

"Uh, wish I could, Cassie, but the real-estate people are coming in the next half hour with a hot prospect. Can I meet you somewhere?"

"I won't get in their way. And I'd love to see the house. Drew has so many childhood memories of it."

"Drew wasn't a child when we bought it."

"Teenage memories, then. Please. It's important."

There was silence on the other end of the line.

"Are you still there, A.W.?"

"Yes."

Cassie's heart sank. She'd been right. "Can I come out, A.W.?"

"The real-estate people are arriving soon, just as I said, Cassie. But not to the house. It's gone. I live in a mobile home now."

Cassie closed her eyes. Poor A.W. Poor Grammy Jo. Poor Drew.

"Stay there," A.W. said. "Now that you know about the house, there's no reason to come here, is there?"

"No."

"Then I'll meet you in the airport restaurant. We need to talk."

"Okay. See you soon. Drive carefully."

"Never." He chuckled.

His response and laughter sounded like the A.W. she'd come to know, and for a moment Cassie thought she must be mistaken about the house. Perhaps he was teasing her about living in a mobile home.

"I'll be there in a jiffy, Cassie," he said. "Goodbye."

No, he wasn't teasing, she realized as all hope disintegrated. What would happen to all of them now?

Cassie found a secluded booth in the restaurant and waited. It was probably the longest forty-five minutes of her life.

A.W. arrived looking as dapper as usual, but his smile was uncertain. Cassie hated having put them both in this position, but didn't Grammy Jo deserve to know her future husband's true financial standing?

"You're looking lovely, Cassie," A.W. said as he took a seat across from her in the booth. "Have you ordered anything?"

"Just my coffee." She indicated the half-full cup of murky liquid in front of her.

"Well, I'm going to have breakfast, and I'd love to buy you some, too."

"That's all right. I—"

"I *can* afford breakfast for both of us, Cassie."

She flushed. "I'm sure you can. I'm not very hungry, that's all."

He looked at her closely. "And you didn't get much

sleep last night, judging from those circles under your eyes. Am I the cause of that?"

"I just want Grammy Jo to be happy, A.W."

"So do I, Cassie. So do I." He signaled the waitress and ordered bacon and eggs for both of them in spite of her murmured protest.

She smiled gently. "That's the sort of thing Drew would do. I guess your grandson inherited some of your high-handedness, A.W." Immediately she regretted her choice of words. "I mean..."

"Cassie." He leaned forward across the table. "It's okay. But you've got to believe that I'm not being high-handed with your grandmother. She knows I'm not particularly rich."

"Does she know you don't own a house anymore?"

"Not quite. But I told her not to expect much out of the sale. I didn't tell her all the gory details because...because I don't want them to get back to Drew. I know that's vain of me, but I've been that boy's idol for so long that I didn't want to disappoint him."

"What happened, A.W.?"

"Cassie, please swear to me you won't tell all this to Drew. I'll reveal all the grisly details to your grandmother, if you insist, but I'd rather not tarnish my image with my grandson, if possible."

Cassie thought of how she could vindicate herself by telling Drew the truth. He'd have to take more notice of her handwriting analysis after discovering she was dead right about his grandfather.

But carrying tales to Drew would crush the spirit in the man sitting across from her and possibly ruin his cherished relationship with his grandson.

"No, A.W. I won't tell him."

"Does he realize you're here?"

"Nobody knows I came. I'm scheduled on the afternoon flight back to Albuquerque, and everyone will think I spent the day at work."

"Thank you for that." He paused as the waitress set their meal in front of them. "And I know I can trust you, Cassie."

"I'm not out to cause any damage, A.W. But I got Grammy Jo into this, and when I suspected that you weren't very well off financially, I began to wonder if..."

"I was marrying Jo for her money?"

"Well...yes."

"I'm not. You've got to believe me."

Cassie wanted to. His piercing gaze reminded her so much of Drew trying to convince her of his love. "Please tell me what happened, A.W."

"I, um, got involved in a few too many games of chance."

"You lost your house because of gambling?"

He took a packet of sugar from the holder and studied it as if he could read the correct answer on the printed label. "I'm afraid so."

Cassie looked at him in alarm. Was Grammy Jo about to marry a compulsive gambler?

"Don't worry. I've come to grips with the problem. It took a few counseling sessions, but I know gambling of any kind is off-limits for me." He creased the top of the sugar packet. "I *did* tell Jo that after she suggested Las Vegas for our honeymoon."

Cassie slumped against the booth. Grammy Jo was knowingly marrying a man who was addicted to gambling. What if he wasn't cured? Albuquerque didn't have any casinos, but there was always the racetrack.

"I can imagine what you're thinking, Cassie. But consider this. All of us have faults. Some drink, some play around, some are inconsiderate boors. Wouldn't you be suspicious if I appeared too perfect? Such people don't exist."

"I suppose not, but this—"

"Is controllable. And I'm controlling it. I figured that Jo has learned enough to warn her away if she wanted to be warned away. But the details about the house, the car, the savings account, are pretty morbid. I hoped never to have to tell anyone about them. I guess you deserve to hear them, though, after traveling all this way to talk to me."

Cassie sat with her arms folded on the table and looked at him for several seconds. Slowly she picked up her fork. "I don't think I want to hear them, after all. Would you please pass the salt?"

A.W. started in surprise. "You're not going to pump me for the whole story?"

"No." She held out the saltshaker. "Care for some?"

A relieved expression spread over his face. "Never touch the stuff. It's bad for you, Cassie."

Cassie smiled. "Grammy Jo keeps telling me the same thing."

"Smart lady."

Cassie held his gaze for a moment. "Yes, I think she is."

After that they spent a pleasant hour together lingering over their coffee and discussing the wedding.

"I have a suggestion for your costume, A.W.," Cassie said at last.

"You do?"

"I think you should dress as a chipmunk."

"A chipmunk? I was planning to be a pirate, with an eye patch and a sword and— Did you say chipmunk?"

"Trust me."

"I know you, Cassie. You have some reason for this. Okay, I'll trust you and be a chipmunk. How's the guest list coming along?"

"Most of our local friends will be there, but we'll have a scarcity of relatives. I think the costume idea is frightening them away. And my folks have scheduled a cruise for that date."

"Spoilsports. Oh, well. We'll have a great time without them, right?"

"Right."

A.W. glanced at his watch. "I'm afraid I do have a few things to accomplish today. Do you want to tag along, or have you planned anything else to take up the time until your plane leaves?"

"As a matter of fact, I'm scheduled to talk with Drew's friend Evan early this afternoon."

A.W. raised an eyebrow questioningly, but when Cassie didn't offer any more information, he didn't pry into her reasons. She had to give him credit for that.

"I'll be glad to take you over to the campus."

"Thanks," Cassie said with a grin. "I guess my heart can stand it."

"I haven't had an accident since I was seventeen."

"I know. Drew insists you're careful. Fast but careful. I'll close my eyes."

"No, I'll drive more slowly."

And to Cassie's surprise he did.

"I just have one question," he said when they were

bidding each other goodbye in front of the psychology building.

"What's that?"

"What finally caused you to come to Phoenix and confront me about this whole business?"

Cassie paused. They'd had a lovely morning together, and if she explained that she'd made the trip on a hunch, they would part amicably. But what if she admitted that she was a graphoanalyst and that she had evaluated the handwriting in his letter to her?

His reaction might very well be like Drew's, and she didn't look forward to that. He'd been completely honest with her, however. If she had insisted, he would have told her anything she wanted to know.

"It started with the cricket story. I had to agree with Grammy Jo about the implausibility of the exterminator excuse. Then it was just little things I put together. The older car, your post-office box, the decision to live in Albuquerque, letting Grammy Jo pay for dinner, letters instead of phone calls."

"Hmm. So on the basis of that, you—"

"No, there's more." Cassie took a deep breath. "I'm a professional graphoanalyst. I wrote you a letter that required an answer. When I got your reply, your handwriting revealed that you were worried about something and that you were quite capable of keeping secrets. I decided to try to uncover them."

"Oh-ho!" He looked at her with new interest. "You analyze handwriting?"

Cassie nodded.

"Fascinating. Tell me, was there any good news in that letter you studied?"

"Of course. I can write it up for you, if you like."

"I certainly would. I've always wanted to have that done. What do you charge?"

"I wouldn't charge you."

"Don't people pay for this sort of thing?"

"Yes, but—"

"Don't you dare consider me a charity case, Cassie. I'm a proud man."

"I know. Your *d* stems show it."

He laughed. "Then let me pay for my analysis."

Cassie kissed him on the cheek. "No way, A.W. I'd never charge family and close friends, and you qualify on both counts."

"Okay, if you're sure that's your reason."

"I'm sure."

"Have you analyzed Drew's handwriting?"

"Uh, yes, I have."

"I'll bet he was really intrigued."

A sharp pain gripped Cassie's heart, but she tried not to reveal her anguish. "Not really," she said, clearing the hoarseness from her voice.

"Couldn't take the heat, huh? I'm surprised, though. Drew's always had such an inquiring mind. I'd think he'd be interested to know about himself."

"He...he doesn't believe my work is valid."

"Oh." A.W. was silent for a moment. "I smell a problem here."

"And now it's your turn to keep a secret, A.W. I don't want my troubles with Drew to spoil Grammy Jo's wedding day. She thinks we're getting along fine, and I'd prefer not telling her otherwise right now. She's crazy about Drew."

"So am I, but it sounds like he's being a little stubborn. I guess he's not old enough to admit he might not know everything."

"I went to him with my study of your letter, and he was furious."

A.W. nodded. "I know he'd defend me to the death. I'm proud of that, but not if it means I'm coming between the two of you."

"You're not," Cassie said quickly. "He wouldn't give credit to my graphoanalysis, no matter who I had studied. I tried to show him my work with Evan's client, who was a problem because he didn't speak or write English. I analyzed his handwriting in his native language, and learned several valuable things about the man. But Drew wouldn't acknowledge that."

"A little overprotective of his own profession, I suspect. Won't you let me have a talk with him?"

"No, please. Besides, he'd soon learn all about this visit of mine, which wouldn't do any of us any good."

A.W. sighed. "Maybe you're right. But I know you two would be great together, if Drew would drop this attitude of his."

"I don't see much chance of that." Cassie touched the older man's arm. "Thanks for listening, anyway. You'd better be on your way."

"True. Incidentally, did you send Evan your findings?"

"Yes. He paid me for my analysis and asked me to call him the next time I was in Phoenix. I think we'll discuss future consulting jobs."

"That's terrific."

"It sure is. I love this work. I wouldn't mind doing it full-time instead of delivering mail."

"Does Drew realize that?"

Cassie shook her head. "No."

"You do love him, don't you?"

Her tone was hesitant. "Yes."

"Then have it out with him. Tell him how important this is to you."

"I haven't the courage, A.W." She opened the car door and paused. "I couldn't bear for him to make fun of my dreams."

12

THE NEXT DAY there was no rose in the mailbox. Cassie told herself it was just as well. In response she removed all the extra junk mail from the bundle she'd been planning to deliver and gave Drew his normal allotment of letters. The rose and the junk mail routine had apparently lost its flavor.

The following weekend Cassie found an apartment. Grammy Jo was too busy to notice whether her granddaughter spent her spare time with Drew or Ruth, and Cassie didn't bother to explain that she'd had no contact with Drew for more than a week.

One by one the roses died. When the last one withered, Cassie felt a desolation like none she'd ever known in her life. It seemed her relationship with Drew was really over at last. All that remained of their time together was the rehearsal and dinner at his house the evening before the wedding, and the wedding itself.

Three days before the wedding A.W. arrived back in town and announced that he'd like to take his bride to Hawaii for their honeymoon. Alarmed about the expense, Cassie cornered him one night when Grammy Jo was still dressing for their dinner date.

"Hawaii?" she whispered.

"The mobile home sold for a much higher price than I'd planned on," he replied in a low tone. "And now that I'm not gambling, it's amazing how far the money goes." He smiled down at her. "Don't worry, Cassie. My travel agent found us a terrific deal, and don't forget that Jo and I qualify for all kinds of discounts if we're willing to admit how old we are."

"I think you'd both better carry proof of age if you expect people to believe you're senior citizens."

"Ugh. There's that term again. I swear I'm going to come up with a better one."

"If you think of one before the wedding ceremony, tell it to the editor of *Inspired Retirement*. She'll probably put it in the story, and you might start something."

"Good idea. And speaking of the wedding, I assume nothing's changed with your problem? I've been pretty involved with Jo, but I haven't noticed any good signs from that grandson of mine."

"Everything's the same. We haven't seen each other since the night before I made the trip to Phoenix."

A.W. shook his head. "Not good. You are still coming to the rehearsal and the dinner at his house tomorrow night?"

"Of course I am."

"I'll be over to pick up both of you in the Audi." He shook his head again. "Can't understand that boy. Maybe I should—"

"No, please don't. Let's both keep our secrets."

A.W. gave her a quick hug. "Okay, Cassie."

THE NEXT EVENING, as Cassie rode to Drew's house with A.W. and Grammy Jo, she wondered how Drew would handle seeing her again. They'd had no contact and no agreement about putting on a good front for their grandparents. Would he continue to do that?

"I don't know why we have to rehearse this thing," Grammy Jo complained. "It's not as if both of us have never done it before. Couldn't we go dancing instead?"

Cassie reached from the back seat to pat her grandmother's shoulder. "I think the bride has the jitters, don't you, A.W.?"

"Could be," the gray-haired man agreed. "Matter of fact, I'm getting a little nervous myself."

"Is that why you're driving so slow?" Grammy Jo asked. "We'll never get there at this rate. Not that I care that much. This rehearsal stuff is for the birds."

"Grammy Jo, weren't you the one who wanted to invite the editor of *Inspired Retirement*?" Cassie asked gently.

"How did I know it would mean all this folderol? How did I know the local television stations would get wind of it and want to film the thing? I've half a mind to elope."

"Don't you dare," Cassie warned. "Not after all the work I've put into my costume. All my friends have, too. My supervisor and his wife are coming as Tweedledee and Tweedledum, if you think that didn't take some work."

Grammy Jo chuckled. "At least they have the shape for it."

"Jo, that's not very nice to say about Cassie's boss and his wife."

"Wait'll you meet them," Grammy Jo advised. "I've never been around such little, roly-poly people in my life. I wonder how he sees over the counter at the post office."

A.W. stopped at a red light and looked at Grammy

Jo with a perfectly straight face. "Haven't you ever heard of a post-office box?" Then he winked at Cassie.

Cassie groaned at the terrible joke, but she was filled with admiration for A.W.'s ability to make any joke at all having to do with a post-office box, considering that that was the vehicle he'd used to guard his embarrassing secret. He was an amazing man.

"Anyway," A.W. continued, "we *won't* elope, will we, Jo?"

Grammy Jo sighed. "I guess not. I've put a lot of work into my costume, too."

"So have I," A.W. agreed with an almost imperceptible glance at Cassie.

She knew then that he'd taken her advice and found a chipmunk costume. How many men would be willing to wear a chipmunk outfit to their own wedding, a wedding that would probably be televised on the ten o'clock news? Would Drew agree to such a thing for her? In her present mood Cassie doubted it.

With A.W. leading the trio, they didn't bother ringing the doorbell when they arrived at Drew's house. They walked right in past the fake cobwebs and the two skeletons hanging on either side of the doorway. An older woman in a suit and a young man in jeans were talking with Drew in the living room, and caterers were at work in the kitchen.

Cassie grabbed the moment before Drew realized they were there to drink in the sight of him. Her gaze roamed eagerly over his thick hair, his straight, almost Grecian nose, his dark beard and mustache, his powerful shoulders. She would always love him, in spite of his behaving like such a turkey.

Then A.W. spoke, and Drew glanced in their direction. He smiled absently at Grammy Jo and A.W., but when his gaze came to rest on Cassie, the smile faded. She couldn't tell at this distance whether the intensity in his eyes signaled pain or pleasure. If he was feeling anything close to the emotions churning inside her, he was experiencing both.

Drew turned to the two people beside him. "Harriet, Jason, let me introduce the bride and groom of this crazy occasion. A. W. Bennett and Jo Reynolds, this is Harriet Stevenson, editor of *Inspired Retirement*, and Jason Cassidy from Channel 7. The young woman behind A.W. and Jo is Jo's granddaughter, Cassie Larue, the maid of honor."

Cassie wondered if she'd imagined the catch in Drew's voice when he'd spoken her name. She felt his attention on her as she shook hands with Harriet and Jason and made polite conversation about the wedding. Jason wasn't staying for the dinner, but he'd asked to watch the rehearsal to plan the story angle.

When Jason somehow became paired with Cassie as the conversation progressed, Drew took a proprietary step toward them and then backed away. Cassie wished he'd asserted himself and acted a tiny bit jealous. It would have helped her state of mind immensely.

But jealousy wasn't part of Drew's personality. She knew that from her in-depth analysis weeks ago. Cassie listened to Jason as if she were enraptured with his discussion of Minicams and voice-overs, but her mind had returned to that first day when she'd seen Drew, when she'd delivered the empty package.

Slowly she relived the cycle of events—the invitation for coffee and the decision to play cupid, the racquetball match, the flight to Phoenix, the magic of their passion mingled with the sharp pain of their disagreement. Cassie remembered her high hopes for an end to that disagreement the day of the balloon ascension and the afternoon of love she and Drew had shared. Since then they had shared only bitterness, and now the story was drawing to a close.

"And what do you do?" Jason asked politely.

The direct question brought Cassie back from her reverie. "Do? I..." She started to give her stock answer that she worked for the post office. Then she glanced at Drew and changed her mind. "I'm a certified graphoanalyst," she said in a voice loud enough for Drew to hear.

Conversation among the other four people in the room ended as Grammy Jo, A.W. and Drew turned to stare at Cassie.

"That's the study of handwriting, isn't it?" Jason pursued. At Cassie's nod he rubbed his chin thoughtfully. "I think you'd make a great interview for one of our talk shows. Would you be interested?"

"Why...why, sure. That sounds like fun." Cassie peeked at Drew and took great satisfaction from his look of astonishment. Her little hobby, indeed! She'd show him.

"How exciting!" Grammy Jo exclaimed, coming over to put an arm around Cassie's waist. "A.W., I don't think I ever told you that Cassie analyzes handwriting."

"Uh, no, you didn't," A.W. said, raising his eyebrows at Cassie.

"Do you have a card so we know where to reach you?" Jason asked.

"No, I don't." She made a mental note. Evan had asked her the same thing. If she intended to bill herself as a professional graphoanalyst, she'd better order some business cards.

"That's okay. Just write your address and phone number in my notebook." Jason pulled a small pad from his hip pocket and handed her a pencil.

"The address will be changing next week, as well as the phone number, so I'll write down both the old and the new," Cassie explained as she gave Jason the information.

Now she really had Drew's attention.

"Sounds like you two had a meeting of the minds," he said casually to them.

"Handwriting experts make terrific talk-show guests," Jason explained.

"And good columnists," Harriet added, joining the conversation. "We've had a handwriting column in the magazine for several months now, and it generates a lot of interest."

Cassie steeled herself for a disparaging word from Drew, but he remained silent. Then she remembered that he hadn't actually voiced his opinion in front of Evan, either.

"Just how do you make money at this?" Jason asked. "Do you write a column, too?"

"Not yet. But I'm pursuing the possibility." It wasn't a fib, she decided. Tonight was her first step. "I charge a fee for a complete analysis, but until recently I've worked only on an individual basis. Not long ago, however, I was put on a retainer by a psychologist in the Phoenix area."

Drew looked stunned.

Cassie hadn't planned this moment. She had expected that at some point Drew would talk to Evan and discover that Cassie had signed an agreement with him, but she hadn't thought the revelation would be so dramatic.

She waited for the feeling of triumph, but instead, sadness crept around her heart and blocked out the bright glow of self-satisfaction. Cassie wanted to share her success with Drew, not parade it righteously in front of him.

"Well, who knows?" Jason said with a smile. "The talk show may bring you some response from local psychologists."

"Both good and bad," Cassie warned him. "Some people in that field are antagonistic to what I do." She couldn't look at Drew.

"Ah, controversy!" Jason exclaimed, rubbing his hands together in delight. "Even better." He thought for a moment and turned a curious eye on Drew. "You told me what you do, but I'm not sure that I—"

Drew sighed. "I'm a psychologist."

"I thought so." Jason's face grew more animated. "Let's see, you're the best man for the wedding, and Cassie's the maid of honor, right?"

"That's right." Drew's jaw flexed under his beard.

"Do you have a working relationship with Cassie?"

"No."

"Are you by chance one of those psychologists who don't approve of—"

"Not at all. I may not have Cassie on a retainer, but the man who does is a friend and colleague. I introduced them. Furthermore, I have the utmost respect for Cassie's work."

Cassie stared in disbelief at Drew's earnest expression. He had to be lying. But that wasn't possible. Drew wasn't capable of distorting the truth like that, especially not with such a convincing look on his face. Or was he? Could her analysis of his handwriting have been wrong?

"I think we'd better get on with the rehearsal, or we'll never eat," A.W. said, putting an arm around Jason's shoulders. "Come on over here, young man, and I'll show you where I'll be standing. The bride will appear from over there, unescorted, we decided. Kind of a chauvinistic practice, this giving away of the bride, don't you think?"

"Uh, yes, I guess so," Jason said, glancing back at Drew and Cassie. His expression revealed that he didn't want to be sidetracked, but neither did he want to offend the distinguished older man who was carefully explaining the mechanics of the wedding.

The rehearsal went smoothly, and at the end of it Cassie found herself on Drew's arm, marching down the area designated as the aisle.

"Interesting about your agreement with Evan," Drew said in an undertone.

"Interesting about your respect for my work," Cassie returned, looking straight ahead. "I can't figure it out. According to my analysis of your writing, you're practically incapable of dishonesty, and yet I know you weren't being truthful."

"Do you?" His grip on her arm tightened.

"I should think so, after all we've been through." The close contact of her arm with his, the touch of his hand covering hers, was making her skin tingle and her head spin.

Grammy Jo approached them with a benevolent smile. "You two look great walking down the aisle together."

Drew released Cassie's arm and put a hand at her waist. "Sounds like a hint, Jo."

"It was." Grammy Jo winked. "This wedding stuff isn't so bad, once you get past the rehearsal part. Let's go eat. The food smells heavenly."

A.W. called from the hallway. "Drew, the whole Bennett crew is at the door, wondering if it's chow time yet. And they're dying to meet the bride. Come over here, Jo."

"Typical mass hysteria," Drew said with a laugh. For a moment he and Cassie were left alone in the midst of the general hubbub. He glanced down at her, and they studied each other for a wordless few seconds. There were many things to be said, but now was not the time to say them. "Ready to meet the rest of the family, including another Andrew W. Bennett?" Drew asked gently.

Cassie took a deep breath. "Two of you have just about taxed my limit."

His brown eyes were understanding. "I'm not surprised. When all this is over—"

"Drew! The caterers can't find the corkscrew!" someone yelled from the other room.

"Coming!" he called. "Cassie, we've got to—"

"You'd better go."

"All right, but you're coming with me." Taking her arm firmly, he propelled her into pandemonium.

The evening was boisterous. Under different circumstances Cassie would have enjoyed it, but her confusion about Drew frustrated her attempts to relax and have a good time. Finally the festivities were over, and some couple, an aunt and uncle of Drew's she thought, was driving her and Grammy Jo home. There hadn't been another chance to talk to Drew all evening. The next day would probably be the same, Cassie decided. After that she wasn't sure if she and Drew would see each other again.

Grammy Jo took Cassie's hand and squeezed it. "You've been a marvelous cupid. Maybe after tomorrow you can do something about your own love life. I think A.W. and I have distracted you and Drew from concentrating on each other."

"That's not true, Grammy Jo."

"I hope you two come to a decision soon, then."

Yes, they probably would, Cassie thought. Once she'd confirmed that Drew hadn't told Jason his true feelings about her work, all hope for a relationship would be gone. It was bad enough that he felt the way he did without having him lie about it.

"Yes, Grammy Jo," she said. "I imagine Drew and I will come to a decision very soon."

THE TELEPHONE AWOKE CASSIE the next morning, but when it stopped ringing she went back to sleep, assuming her grandmother had answered it.

Moments later Grammy Jo tapped on her door. "Cassie? It's Drew, sweetheart."

Cassie reached for the phone with trepidation. Did he want to clarify their situation now, before the wedding? "Hello, Drew," she said as casually as possible.

"Keep your voice low, Cassie. Don't let Jo hear you. It appears that Gramps has run off somewhere."

13

CASSIE CONTROLLED HERSELF with difficulty. "What do you mean, run off?" she asked with low urgency. "My God, Drew, this is—"

"I know. He left me a note saying to cancel the wedding. All his stuff is still here, so I think he went somewhere close by to brood. Any ideas?"

Cassie thought quickly. If A.W. had suddenly got cold feet, it probably had something to do with the worry about his gambling secrets, but she'd pledged not to reveal anything she knew.

"Cassie, I know how I reacted to your analysis of his handwriting, but if anything you learned can help us now, either to find him or understand why he's doing this, I'd appreciate it."

She closed her eyes in response to his plea, knowing how much it must have cost him to make it. "I'll do what I can, Drew. What time is it?"

"Nine-fifteen."

"Wow, did I oversleep."

"Me, too. That was quite a party last night. I woke up a little while ago and found the note on my bedside table."

"Okay, if it's that late, I have an idea where he might have gone. The Tramway opens at nine."

"You think he went up there? How could you know that from his handwriting?"

In spite of her tension, Cassie smiled. "This guess has nothing to do with handwriting. I just remember that he loves heights. He took us to lunch at a restaurant overlooking Phoenix, and he was crazy about the balloon ride. He seemed to enjoy the tram and the restaurant up there. I think he's on top of Sandia Peak."

"Good reasoning," he said with admiration. "I'll pick you up in twenty minutes."

"Me?"

"I need your help, Cassie. I think...that you know him better than I do. I want to make sure he doesn't commit a monumental error by calling off this wedding."

Cassie couldn't argue. After all, she did know some things about A.W. that Drew didn't. And Grammy Jo's happiness was on the line. "All right. I'll be ready."

"WHAT AN IMPETUOUS MAN," she gushed to Grammy Jo as she whirled out of her room fifteen minutes later. "He insists on taking me out to breakfast."

"How nice." Grammy Jo smiled serenely.

Cassie turned away from the joy on her grandmother's face. If she and Drew didn't find A.W. and convince him to come back for the wedding, Grammy Jo's hopes for a wonderful future would be dashed. "I'll be back in plenty of time to help you with the chipmunk costume," she said, grabbing a coat from the hall closet as the doorbell rang. It would be mighty chilly on that mountain. And not just because of the weather.

"Thanks for coming," Drew said, helping her into the car.

"I have a big stake in this, too."

As they drove toward the base of the mountain, he

spoke first. "Why didn't you tell me you went to Phoenix?"

"Why should I have?" Cassie bristled. "I take it you've talked to Evan."

"I called him last night, or I should say this morning, after the party."

"But that must have been after three!"

"I figured he deserved to be hauled out of bed for not telling me about your agreement. After all, he knows how I feel about you."

And how is that? Cassie longed to ask. "He also knows how you feel about graphoanalysis. I doubt that he was anxious to bring up that touchy subject again."

"Well, I brought it up when I called."

"I'll bet you did. He must have loved that at three in the morning." Cassie could imagine Drew's ridiculing Evan's decision to put her on a retainer.

"He did. I apologized for being such a nerd."

Several seconds ticked by as Cassie looked at him, dumbfounded. "You what?"

He glanced at her with a half smile. "Ah-ha, I've startled you as much as you did me with your announcement last night. Touché, my love."

"Drew, I don't under—"

"Don't you?" His tone was light, almost teasing. "I thought you were the lady with the answers. Don't tell me you can't predict my behavior after all that study of my handwriting."

"What do you mean?"

"Okay, so I've got a heavy stroke. I do have a tendency to dig my heels in, hold on to a cherished prejudice. But I also have those inverted wedges, which indicates an exploratory mind, right?"

"I never told you that."

"Is it true?"

"Yes, but..." Cassie gasped as realization dawned. "You've been studying graphoanalysis."

"Reluctantly at first, but recently I've been very diligent."

"I don't believe it."

"It's all in the wedges, Cassie. I had to find out about this topic that had caused all the trouble between us."

"And?" She held her breath.

"And the more I read, the more fascinated I become. I was ready to talk about it the night you revealed your doubts about Gramps, but when you turned your analysis on someone I loved..."

"I probably shouldn't have dragged you into it, but I had no one else to consult."

"And I came unglued."

"You sure did."

"I didn't want to believe what you were suggesting. I still don't. But maybe...maybe there is something to all this stuff about brain writing."

Cassie let out her breath slowly.

"Did you know," Drew continued, "that if someone loses the use of his hands and starts writing with his feet, his script stays basically the same?"

"Yes." Cassie grinned. Drew was hooked.

He glanced at her. "I see that triumphant smile, Cassie Larue," he taunted, but then his voice softened. "And you deserve to wear it. I owe you an apology. I owe you more than that, but the apology is all we have time for right now."

At his humble sincerity Cassie's eyes filled with tears. "Drew, I..."

"Hey, don't cry." He reached for her hand and laced his fingers through hers. "I know you've got a high emotional response level, which I happen to be crazy about, but we have a job to do this morning. Then we'll have time for us. But I probably won't let you cry then, either. I have a much better activity for you to consider."

Cassie sniffled. "You've been analyzing my handwriting, too? You don't even have a sample."

"Sure I do. That day you gave me your grandmother's address, remember?"

"You kept that?"

He shrugged. "As you also know, I'm a tad bit sentimental."

"I know." Cassie dabbed at her eyes with a tissue. "The roses were lovely, Drew."

"They were sent by a nerd. When I was giving you the roses, I still didn't understand your obsession with graphoanalysis. It wasn't until we had that fight about Gramps that I figured out I'd better hit the books or risk losing you forever."

"I don't know what to say."

He winked. "I'll help you think of something later. In the meantime, we've got to concentrate on Gramps. You saw him in Phoenix, too, didn't you?"

"Yes. But, Drew, I can't—"

"I'm not asking you to tattle and reveal everything you found out. Whatever it is, he has to tell me. But that's not a requirement, either. Mostly I'd like to see these two people married and headed for Hawaii. It would be good for them, and—" he sent her a look of frustrated passion "—good for us."

"Let's hope he's on top of that mountain," Cassie said fervently as they neared the tram terminal.

Drew squeezed her hand. "Let's hope so."

He was. They knew it the moment they spied his battered MG parked in the Tramway lot. They waited anxiously for the next red car to glide down the mountain on its thick cable. Quickly they leaped aboard.

As the tram docked, they spotted him immediately—a stately figure braced against the wind, which whipped his gray hair and the flap of his trench coat as he stood alone on the observation deck. He didn't notice their approach.

"Nice view," Drew remarked when they were beside him.

A.W. turned, and his eyes registered a moment's surprise before he glanced back at the panorama spread before them. "Yep."

Cassie shifted impatiently from one foot to the other as they stood silently together. She wanted to grab A.W. by the scuff of the neck and drag him back to Grammy Jo, but the situation called for a little more tact than that. What was the right thing to say in a case like this?

It *was* a nice view, she thought as the silence dragged on. She wished the three of them were there merely to enjoy it. The aspens had turned color, splashing the mountainside with gold and making the pines look even greener in contrast. Beyond the city the bluffs were the same pink and purple shades that Cassie remembered from her morning plane ride with Drew.

Finally A.W. spoke. "You two had coffee yet?"

"No," Cassie replied immediately, grasping at the first opportunity for communication.

"Come on. I'm buying."

The ride back down the mountain was another marathon of stoic silence.

"Follow me," A.W. said, hopping into his MG and tearing out of the parking lot.

"Here goes nothing," Drew said as they threw themselves into the Audi and Drew peeled out after his grandfather. Cassie gripped the armrest and prayed they'd all arrive at a restaurant soon without a police escort.

Fortunately for all of them, Albuquerque's finest didn't show up on the pell-mell ride to the coffee shop that A.W. selected. He stood by the tiny green car, smiling for the first time since they'd encountered him. "Wasn't that exciting?"

"No," Cassie and Drew chorused at once.

"You guys aren't any fun. Jo would have loved it." He paused for a minute and then shook his head. "Let's get some coffee."

They ended up with more than coffee after A.W. proclaimed that Cassie and Drew looked like hell and should be taking better care of themselves.

"It's time you two got married," he said in a loud voice that caused several of the restaurant's patrons to turn and stare. "Look at you. You're both a mess."

"I agree," Drew said, taking Cassie's hand under the table. "But we're here because this is supposed to be your wedding day, not ours. And you don't look so great yourself."

"Don't feel so great, either." He gave Drew a piercing look. "That little gal there loves you more than you deserve. Told me so in Phoenix. Also told me enough about your behavior that I decided you have mush for brains."

"A.W.," Cassie began, "I thought we—"

"The time for secrets is over, Cassie," A.W. said, interrupting her. "That's what I decided on the mountain before you two arrived. First I intend to tell Drew everything, and I mean everything, and then I'm going over to Jo's house and confess that I varnished the truth with her, too. After she throws me out, I'll go back to Phoenix, I guess. Although I don't have a place to live anymore."

"Whoa, back up there." Drew laid a hand on his grandfather's sleeve. "Let's take this slower. What did Cassie tell you in Phoenix?"

"Said she loved you, you turkey. Beats me why."

Drew turned to Cassie. "You did?"

She nodded.

Drew's eyes glowed with happiness. "Hallelujah," he said softly, looking at her as if he'd just been confronted with a miracle. "And you're right, Gramps. I don't deserve her love, as pigheaded as I've been."

A.W. chortled with glee. "You admit it? Well, that's a beginning."

"This is a day for beginnings." Drew's gaze lingered on the dimples that played hide-and-seek with him as Cassie's smile flickered over her lips, lips that he longed to taste again and again. But now was not the time. With great reluctance he returned his attention to his recalcitrant grandfather. "So what's the terrible secret you've been hiding from me, Gramps?"

A.W.'s voice quavered as he began the sad story of the past two years.

Cassie's heart went out to the man as he haltingly

and painstakingly explained his financial downfall to his grandson. Drew's eyes glistened by the end of the story, and A.W. had to clear his throat several times.

"I'm sorry, Gramps. It must have been horrible for you."

"What's horrible is facing you with the truth. Now that's horrible."

"But you've conquered it, this gambling fever. That's something to be proud of."

"I've let you down, Drew. All your life you've looked up to me. I know that. And now..." A.W. pushed his food aimlessly around his plate.

"I still look up to you, Gramps."

A.W. raised his head, and the two men exchanged a long, meaningful look. A.W.'s voice was husky. "Thank you, Drew."

Cassie fumbled for her coffee cup and drank the last of its cold contents in an effort to keep from crying. She figured if she started, both men would have a bigger struggle keeping their emotions in check, and everyone would be embarrassed.

"And now it's time to go see Jo, if you two will excuse me," A.W. said, standing and surreptitiously dabbing at his eyes with a napkin. "But I'll come back to the house before I leave, Drew, to get my stuff."

"Don't jump to any conclusions about Grammy Jo," Cassie said, rising from the table. "I predict there will be a wedding yet."

"That would be nice," A.W. said, "but I couldn't blame her if she called the whole thing off. She's a classy lady, and this is not a pretty story."

Cassie reached up to give him a hug. "No, but you're a classy guy."

"Who is also picking up the check," A.W. said, grabbing the ticket from their table.

"Gramps, you already paid a lot for this meal," Drew said quietly, holding out his hand. "At least let the small part be on me."

A.W. looked at him for a minute as if weighing the principles involved. "All right," he said slowly, putting the bill in Drew's outstretched hand. "Thank you."

"My pleasure."

"I'll call you when Jo and I have reached a decision," A.W. said. "Where will you two be?"

"At my house," Drew said firmly, taking Cassie's elbow.

"Do you want me to help you set up for the wedding?" Cassie asked as they drove away from the restaurant.

Drew glanced at her. "Not on your life."

"But there must be lots more to do before seven tonight."

"There sure is." He cut quickly through the morning traffic, driving almost as fast as his grandfather usually did.

"And there will be a wedding. I have no doubt that Grammy Jo will forgive that man anything and the ceremony will take place as planned. The decorations aren't all in place—at least they weren't last night."

"Still aren't."

"Fortunately, all the pumpkins were carved during the party, although tipsy people wielding knives made me very nervous. Are the orange and black streamers up yet?"

"Nope." He zoomed through a yellow light.

"Drew, you act as if you don't care about the preparations for this wedding."

"It's not the most pressing issue right now."

"When do the caterers arrive?"

"Five o'clock." The tires of the Audi squealed as he cut the corner and headed down his street.

"Oh."

"And that's when I start decorating."

"Oh. Is anybody at your house right now?"

"Nope."

Shivers of anticipation rippled over her as his purpose, which she had suspected earlier, became clear.

"Aren't you going to ask what I plan to do between now and five o'clock?" he asked, swerving into the drive.

"Organize your costume?" she ventured, smiling.

"What I have in mind requires no costume at all."

She glanced at him, suddenly shy after all their days apart. "I see."

He turned off the ignition. "I hope so. Because I'm not sure we'll make it out of the car and through the front door before I grab you. If we're extremely lucky, we'll make it to the bedroom. Get the picture?"

She nodded.

"I love you."

"And I love you," she whispered.

They made it into Drew's bedroom, but most of their clothes didn't. By the time they toppled onto his unmade bed, they had discarded the last barrier between them. Greedily hands reached and mouths sought in a frenzy of renewal.

"God, you taste good," Drew said with a gasp, returning to kiss a turgid breast after paying moist tribute to all the secret places that he loved.

"And you feel wonderful," Cassie murmured, kneading the firm muscles of his back and thighs. Saving the best for last, she boldly caressed his velvet shaft, bringing a groan of joy from his lips and a rush of desire to her own pulsing center. "I want you," she said in a voice thick with passion.

"Soon."

"Now," she demanded, stroking him relentlessly.

With a low, animal sound from deep in his throat, he spread her thighs with his knee and thrust forward.

A sound that was partly a sigh, partly a moan came from her parted lips as she arched upward.

"You're home now, Cassie," he murmured against her ear. "The search is over."

"Yes," she whispered, wrapping her arms around him and entwining her legs with his.

Holding her just as tightly as she held him, Drew lay still for a moment. Then gradually, in tune with each other, they began to move, undulating together, increasing the tempo until their heartbeats thundered in their ears.

Cassie thought of the moments in the plane with Drew, of the abandoned rolling, the climbing. Then she thought no more as sensation took her into a breathless ascent.

Their bodies shook with the force of that final moment when their souls burst free and danced wildly to the primitive beat known only to those who are helplessly, hopelessly in love.

IF THE FILM CLIPS on the ten o'clock news were any indication, the wedding was a complete success. The camera operator caught the best man's startled expression when the maid of honor appeared in a World War I pilot's costume very similar to his.

The crepe-paper streamers looked straight, giving no indication that they'd been hastily attached by two lovers who stopped often to kiss each other. Cobwebs drifted from the corners of the room, and cardboard bats clung to the walls.

During the ceremony the camera panned the seated guests, focusing on the short, round figures of Tweedledee and Tweedledum, a fierce gorilla, several pirates, two incredibly ugly witches, a few ghosts—one in a flowered sheet—and a tall brunette in an exotic gypsy costume.

The final shot of the segment included two chipmunks in a fond embrace, the voice-over announcing that these two people had spurned the label "senior citizens" and preferred to think of themselves as "elegant elders."

At the conclusion of the news coverage, the assembled guests stomped, cheered and whistled their approval. The bride and groom, however, saw neither the telecast nor their guests' reaction to it. They were enjoying their own quiet celebration of love in Grammy Jo's new king-sized water bed. On a table nearby lay two airline tickets for the next day's flight to Hawaii.

The wedding guests didn't seem to mind that the two people responsible for the party had left them to their own devices. Plenty of food and drink remained, and the music was perfect for dancing. The guests stayed on. And on.

"I think it's the costumes," Drew said, putting an

arm around Cassie and drawing her into a relatively quiet corner. "People feel more like partying when they're wearing costumes. They lose their inhibitions."

"I don't know about inhibitions, but the gorilla's lost an ear, and that witch's wig is slipping."

"That witch is a he, and he just finished doing time for mail fraud."

"Oh, *he's* the one. He's dancing with the postmaster's wife, in case you didn't notice."

"I noticed. Or is he dancing with the postmaster? In those Tweedledee and Tweedledum outfits I can't tell them apart."

"I hope the mail-fraud witch can. Ruth looks great in her gypsy costume."

"Not as great as my World War I flying ace." Drew sighed. "I wish they'd all go home."

"That's not very hospitable of you."

He rubbed the small of her back. "I don't feel hospitable. I want to take you back to bed. Jo and Gramps have all the luck."

"It's their wedding." Cassie leaned into the persuasive massage he was giving her. "Mmm, that's nice."

"I can imagine something nicer. Aren't you hot in that costume?"

"If I'm not now, I will be soon."

"Good. Think anybody would notice if we ducked into the bedroom and—"

"Yes. My supervisor is here, remember?"

"So what? You won't be a postal employee much longer. Your alternate career is launched."

"I hope so, Drew."

"It is. The talk show will help, and I have a few contacts in the psychology field, don't forget."

She glanced up in surprise. "You'd promote me? I didn't realize you were that committed to graphoanalysis."

"I'm that committed to you." He brushed her lips gently. "God, this house it too damn full of people."

Cassie laughed. "Shall we yell 'fire' and clear the place out?"

"Sounds like an excellent idea," he murmured, sipping lazily at her lips. "When we get married, let's not invite anyone except Jo and Gramps. They'll have sense enough to leave us alone."

"Are we getting married?"

"We'd better be because you caught that bouquet of black orchids Jo tossed, and I'm not letting some other guy into line ahead of me."

Cassie smiled at him. "I'm not surprised. After all, you have very firm downstrokes."

"And that's true of my handwriting, as well."

She chuckled. "You're a rogue, Drew Bennett."

"Yep. Is it yes or no?"

She framed his face with her hands, loving the soft brush of his beard against her palm. "Yes."

His eyes blazed with joy. "Hot dog. Excuse me a minute." Drew left her standing in the corner, wondering what crazy thing her dashing pilot would do next.

He turned off the music in the middle of a song and made a megaphone of his two hands. "Attention, please, everyone! It's been a great party, but the time has come for all you lovely people to go home."

There was a moment of shocked surprise, and then the guests began dutifully gathering their belongings and straggling out the door.

"See you at work tomorrow," Tweedledum said to Cassie as he left with Tweedledee.

"She won't be able to make it," Drew answered before Cassie could open her mouth. "As a matter of fact, she'll be quitting soon to become a full-time graphoanalyst."

"A what?" Tweedledum peered up at Drew.

"She analyzes handwriting," Drew explained. "It's a very useful tool for deciphering personality traits. Did you know that—"

"Drew," Cassie interrupted gently, "everyone else has left."

"They have? Terrific. Wish I could explain more about this handwriting business," he said, ushering Tweedledum and Tweedledee out the door, "but I have some analyzing of my own to do right now."

"Of what?" Cassie asked, laughing as she leaned against the closed door.

He pulled her close. "I thought we could study my downstrokes," he said, covering her mouth with his.

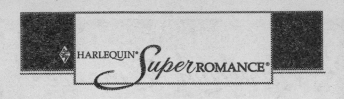

...there's more to the story!

Superromance.
A *big* satisfying read about unforgettable characters. Each month we offer *six* very different stories that range from family drama to adventure and mystery, from highly emotional stories to romantic comedies—and much more! Stories about people you'll believe in and care about. Stories too compelling to put down....

Our authors are among today's *best* romance writers. You'll find familiar names and talented newcomers. Many of them are award winners— and you'll see why!

If you want the biggest and best in romance fiction, you'll get it from Superromance!

Emotional, Exciting, Unexpected...

HARLEQUIN®
Makes any time special ®

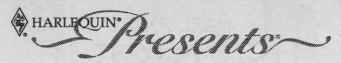

HARLEQUIN Presents

**The world's bestselling romance series...
The series that brings you your favorite authors,
month after month:**

Helen Bianchin...Emma Darcy
Lynne Graham...Penny Jordan
Miranda Lee...Sandra Marton
Anne Mather...Carole Mortimer
Susan Napier...Michelle Reid

and many more uniquely talented authors!

Wealthy, powerful, gorgeous men...
Women who have feelings just like your own...
The stories you love, set in exotic, glamorous locations...

HARLEQUIN Presents

Seduction and passion guaranteed!

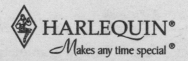

From rugged lawmen and valiant knights to defiant heiresses and spirited frontierswomen, Harlequin Historicals will capture your imagination with their dramatic scope, passion and adventure.

*Harlequin Historicals...
they're too good to miss!*